Brendan tumbled backward. His arms flailed, but he couldn't regain his balance with Boffo's weight pressing into him.

Brendan's legs shot out from under him, and down he went, along with Boffo. The plant flew up out of his hand and landed on Matthew's head at the same time Brendan's back thumped to the ground. He exhaled with an "oof" as Boffo bounced on his chest.

Brendan struggled for breath with the huge dog sprawled on top of him. Brendan was trapped. Nothing would move Boffo if Boffo didn't want to be moved.

Ashley squealed with glee, then giggled. The shrill sound prompted Boffo into high gear. His tongue flashed out toward Brendan's face.

"No!" Brendan gasped, calling out as he raised his arms, but he was too late to protect himself from the onslaught of Boffo's sloppy doggy kisses.

Ashley appeared beside them. "Him loves you!" she sang as she danced in a circle, waving her arms above her head and spinning around on her toes.

Still atop the desk, with her elbows fixed on the hard surface, Shanna leaned forward and buried her face in her palms.

The man was never going to get her landscaping done. Either that or he was going to quit, and it would be all her fault.

She didn't want him to leave. Not just for the job he was doing, and not for herself.

Despite the havoc, her children hadn't had such fun with a man since. . .Shanna couldn't remember.

GAIL SATTLER lives on the wet West Coast, where you don't have to shovel rain, with her husband, three sons, two dogs, five lizards, one toad, and a degu named Bess. For three years in a row Gail was voted number one Favorite Heartsong Author, then was initiated into the Heartsong Authors Hall of Fame. Gail loves to read stories with a happy ending, which is why she writes them. Visit Gail's Web site at www.gailsattler.com.

Books by Gail Sattler

HEARTSONG PRESENTS

Don't miss out on any of our super romances. Write to us at the following address for information on our newest releases and club information.

Heartsong Presents Readers' Service
PO Box 721
Uhrichsville, OH 44683

Or visit www.heartsongpresents.com

Love
by the Yard

Gail Sattler

Heartsong Presents

A note from the Author:
I love to hear from my readers! You may correspond with me by writing:

Gail Sattler
Author Relations
PO Box 721
Uhrichsville, OH 44683

ISBN 978-1-59789-455-5

LOVE BY THE YARD

Our mission is to publish and distribute inspirational products offering exceptional value and biblical encouragement to the masses.

PRINTED IN THE U.S.A.

one

"Hey! Come back here with that!"

Shanna McPherson cringed at the sound of her land-scaper's angry voice. A loud crash immediately followed the outburst.

She winced, hoping against hope, waiting to hear Boffo bark. But he didn't.

The only reason he wouldn't bark would be because he had something in his mouth. Which meant that Boffo was up to more mischief.

Shanna peeked out of the window above her desk, over the expanse of torn-up grass, mounds of debris, rocks, broken cement, and piles of dirt, trying to see what the trouble was this time.

"Mommy, is Boffo being bad again?"

Shanna sighed, almost welcoming the distraction from her four-year-old daughter, who was playing with her stuffed toys on the floor beside her desk, as she did every day while Shanna worked. "Yes, Ashley, he is."

Ashley squealed and jumped to her feet. "I'm gonna see what he's got!"

"No, Ashley," Shanna said as she began pushing her chair out from behind the desk. "Mommy will. . ."

Shanna didn't complete her sentence. Ashley was already outside.

"Boffo! Boffo! You can't do that!" Ashley yelled as she ran, waving her tiny arms in the air, running toward Boffo from one direction while the landscaper chased him from the other. As Boffo ran, something Shanna couldn't identify dangled from Boffo's mouth.

Shanna sprinted from the cement patio onto what once was grass, but her feet sank unevenly in the loose mud, slowing her too much to catch her daughter or her dog. "Ashley!" she yelled, louder than she probably should have. "Come back here! Mommy will get whatever Boffo took!"

She finally caught up to Ashley at the same time her landscaper caught up with Boffo.

He held Boffo firmly by the collar, halting the wayward canine's movement. "You mangy mutt," he ground out from between clenched teeth while his closed fist moved toward Boffo's face.

Shanna gasped. "Stop! He's just. . ."

The man opened his hand directly in front of Boffo's nose, displaying a large dog biscuit.

Without hesitation or guilt, Boffo dropped his prize and latched onto the offering, his tail wagging, completely oblivious to the disruption he'd caused.

Mr. Gafferty didn't wait for the crunching to stop. He immediately scooped his tool up from the ground. Just as Shanna bent down to hold Ashley, the landscaper turned around and saw them.

He froze for a moment, then stiffened to his full height. "Your dog still seems to think this is a big game, Mrs. McPherson."

Shanna looked up at Brendan Gafferty. Way up.

She'd always considered him tall, but from her position near the ground, Brendan seemed like Paul Bunyan.

Slowly, Shanna rose to her feet.

At her full height, he towered above her by about a

foot—which meant that Brendan was six feet five inches tall. The only thing about him that wasn't like Paul Bunyan was his hair; Brendan's was dark blond. Yet he did have a well-manicured beard and neatly trimmed mustache. Also like Paul Bunyan, Brendan had broad shoulders with a he-man physique to match. He was even wearing a red plaid shirt, the sleeves rolled up to his elbows. He didn't have a huge ax, but he was holding some kind of pointy gardening tool in his hand. All that was missing was the blue ox.

Shanna wanted to back up, but she didn't want to let him see that he made her nervous. She looked up at him as he looked down at her. "I'm so sorry about Boffo," she said. "I don't know what I'm going to do with him."

Brendan raised his free hand to his head, as if he were going to run his fingers through his hair; but a few inches before he actually touched his hair, his hand froze. He studied his hand, rubbed his fingers together, then lowered his arm to his side. "I don't know, either. Yesterday, when you tied him up, I'd never heard a dog make a noise like that before. I thought he was going to die or something. Then, when one of your neighbors yelled at him to shut up, he yowled even louder."

Ashley nodded repeatedly. "His feelings was very hurt. Boffo doesn't like to get tied up."

Shanna's cheeks burned as she remembered the incident. Most of her neighbors were amused by Boffo's antics until he started making too much noise, as he had yesterday. "I don't know what gets into him. He's fine on a leash, but if the dog chain comes out, he goes crazy."

As if he knew they were talking about him, Boffo returned. He sat in front of Brendan, raised one paw, and brushed it against Brendan's jeans, leaving a huge black smear extending from midthigh to just below his knee.

"If you want another biscuit, forget it, dog. They're reserved for the next time I need to bribe you." He patted his pocket. "This hasn't been a good day. I don't have many left, and it's not even lunchtime yet."

Shanna checked her watch. It was 9:57, which meant she had an hour and thirteen minutes to do three hours' worth of work before she had to pick up her son, Matthew, from kindergarten.

She reached for her daughter's hand. "Come on, Ashley. Let's go into the house. The nice man has a lot to do, and we're keeping him from his work."

Ashley's eyes widened as she looked up at her mother. "But what about Boffo?"

All three heads turned at the same time. Boffo was gone. He had moved quietly to the corner of the yard, where he was in the process of digging a hole in the soft, freshly dug dirt. As they watched, he dropped something into the hole, then began to cover his prize by pushing the dirt back into the hole with his nose.

"No! Not again!" Brendan yelled as he took off at a run toward the dog.

Ashley squealed, clapped her hands, and danced in one spot.

"Boffo! No!" Shanna yelled, running behind Brendan.

Brendan pushed Boffo away with one hand while he brushed away the mud with his other one. He pulled up a dirty, but otherwise undamaged, roll of some kind of rubber product that Shanna couldn't identify.

He released the dog and shook the dirt from what he'd recovered.

Shanna stared at what looked like a piece of a rolled-up

mat, something she couldn't see a use for outside of the bathroom. "What is that?" she asked.

He brushed off the last clump of mud. "It's bark wrap. I brought a few rolls today to put around the base of your trees. It's a way to protect them when I'm digging and using the rototiller. I can protect your trees from me, but I can't seem to protect them from your dog."

She turned to stare at Boffo, who was sitting beside the mess from the freshly dug hole, his tongue lolling from his mouth, happy as could be. The dog wasn't bothered at all that his plan had been foiled and his buried treasure had been taken from him.

"I think I'll have to take him in the house." Shanna cringed inwardly as she spoke. Since Brendan had dug up what was left of her pathetic grass in the backyard, Boffo's feet were always muddy. Today, with both Boffo and Brendan digging, his feet were even worse than usual.

She didn't have enough time as it was, but now she had to bathe the dog. Otherwise, she would have to add ruined carpeting to the growing list of everything else Boffo had destroyed—inside and out—since she'd hired Brendan to fix her yard.

She glanced at the house. She didn't want to think of what Boffo would do once he figured out that he was locked inside. The day before yesterday, when she'd tried to restrict his access to Brendan's work, he'd gone berserk. Boffo had burst through the screen door, creating a gaping hole. Fortunately, Brendan happened to have a piece of screen in his truck, so he'd fixed it. However, the process had taken more time from what he was really there for, which was to make her yard fit for her clients to see as they passed through it to get to her office in the back of her house.

Brendan turned toward his truck, then back to Shanna. "I know you don't like to close the big door, but I used the last of my screen the other day. I don't know if it's such a great idea to put him inside. Is it possible to leave him at a friend's house or something?"

Shanna couldn't fault the man for being frustrated with her ditzy dog. As a professional landscaper, Brendan had other clients, and Boffo's antics had put him behind schedule. "I've already asked around. No one is volunteering."

She couldn't afford to put Boffo in a boarding kennel. She could barely afford the landscaping, but it was a must. She couldn't make ends meet just taking on residential customers who only needed her to do their income tax in the spring. She needed to contract out to businesses that required accounting work done throughout the entire year, which meant competing with the services that had their offices in the expensive high-rises downtown.

She'd taken a number of potential clients whom she'd needed to impress through her house on the way to her office. Not that her house was messy, but she did have two small children. Instead of giving them a professional tour, she'd looked like a harried single mother trying to earn a few bucks in an extra room.

They'd taken their business elsewhere. Shanna couldn't afford for that to happen again. To get ahead, she had to present herself as a professional accountant with an efficient home office.

The room she'd converted into an office was on the ground level at the rear of the house, so she'd hired a contractor to create a door leading directly outside. That way, no one would have to go through the living area of her house to get to her office. It had been a tremendous expense, but it worked, creating a professional separation between home and office. The next step was to make the entrance through the yard look professional, which was why she'd hired Brendan Gafferty.

If he could get the job done in spite of her children—and her dog.

Ashley wrapped her arms around Shanna's leg. "Mommy, please don't take Boffo to Uncle Ray's house to play with Killer!"

Brendan suddenly stopped shaking the dirt off his bark wrap. "Killer?" He looked down at Ashley. "That doesn't sound like your average house pet."

Shanna squatted rather indelicately, wanting to speak to Ashley at eye level but not wanting to kneel in the mud. "No, Ashley, we won't do that. Killer isn't very friendly." She looked up at Brendan. "Killer is a pit bull and rottweiler cross. My brother-in-law keeps him as a watchdog, but he's not trained; he's just mean. I don't consider him safe around Boffo, even though Boffo is bigger. I especially don't trust him around the children." She'd seen her brother-in-law in action around his dog. He was unkind to Killer on purpose, to keep the animal agitated. The worst part was that Ray was proud of it.

"It's okay, Mrs. McPherson. I'll figure out something. Besides, Boffo has been pretty active since I got here. He's got to be ready for a nap soon. I hope."

She knew Boffo wouldn't sleep if she bathed him. He would only run around more than usual because he was wet.

For now, Brendan was being very patient. Shanna didn't know how long that would last or what would happen when he reached the end of his tolerance.

She stood. "I can't leave him out here to annoy you any

more than he already has. I think it's best for me to take him inside and see if he'll sleep." Dirty or not. She could always wash Boffo's blanket. The carpet probably needed steam cleaning anyway. "We have to go, Ashley. It's almost time to pick up your brother, and I still have lots of work to do. Come on, Boffo. You, too."

❧

Brendan stood with his fists resting on his hips as Shanna McPherson led her daughter and her wayward dog across the uneven surface of the yard, slogging through the mud, before they all disappeared into the house.

He'd done a lot of residential work, but he'd never had a project like this one.

He should have known something wasn't quite right. After he accepted the contract, his friend Harry, who happened to be Shanna's pastor, offered to pray for things to go well. Then he'd thanked Brendan for his kindness in agreeing to do the work.

It wasn't kindness. It was a job.

Or at least it was at first.

Initially, Brendan had given Shanna McPherson a reduced rate because she went to his friend's church. However, the reduced rate became even more reduced when the job didn't go quite as planned. Already, he'd spent too much time trying to outmaneuver her daffy dog and find ways to put her kids to work when Shanna was busy in her office.

He continued to stare at the closed door.

Quitting wasn't an option. Besides giving his word that he would finish the job, to make things even more complicated, Harry had told Brendan a few things he really didn't want to know.

The life insurance and protection on the mortgage payment were void when her husband died, something she'd discovered the hard way. Because she hadn't worked outside her home since before her kids were born, she couldn't find a job that paid well enough to support herself and her family and still pay the mortgage. The small accounting business that she ran out of her home wasn't enough. In a last-ditch effort, she had used the last of her savings for renovations. If that didn't work to generate enough new business, she would have to sell the house.

Thinking of what Harry said made Brendan remember his childhood in painful detail. Brendan knew what it was like to need help, watching his world crumble around him, praying and hoping for something good to happen. His gut churned, knowing the same thing was happening to Shanna and her little family.

Brendan's father had died when Brendan was a young boy. Like Shanna, his mother struggled to support them when he was too young to understand the big picture and all the hardships. Only by the grace of God and the goodness and generosity of the people in their church had they come out relatively unscathed. Through it all, his mother had taught him two important lessons: The first was to trust in God, no matter what. The second was that God's way to return a favor was to pass it on.

The way things were going, by the time he finished, his profit margin would be so slim that landscaping Shanna McPherson's yard would indeed be a favor. All he could do was chalk it up to the Lord's work and finish cheerfully.

He sighed, then returned to his task, which he now could do uninterrupted—at least until Shanna brought her son home from school. Then the boy would want to help.

Today, though, Brendan could give the boy something genuinely useful to do. Matthew could fill in the hole the dog had made.

Instead of dwelling on everything that had gone wrong, Brendan rolled up his sleeves and set to work on digging up more rocks and boulders, then painstakingly moving them to their designated locations. He intended to use them to make rock gardens, which, according to their agreed plans, would be on top of two boulders in the yard that jutted out above ground level. When the house was originally constructed, the contractor had left them where they were in the backyard, not quite buried. Without the proper equipment, which was very expensive to hire in, Brendan couldn't dig them out and remove them. Nor could he dig underneath them to bury them all the way. All he could do was put more rocks on top and grow something in the pile to make it look like he'd done it on purpose.

After he rolled one more boulder into place, he smiled with self-satisfaction, mentally picturing what it was going to look like once he packed in some good soil, planted flowers in it, then surrounded his artwork with ground cover shrubs. He had big plans for this yard, regardless of the price he was doing it for.

He was going to do a good job, despite "helpful" kids and a digging dog.

Halfway through digging up another boulder, the door opened. Shanna and Ashley walked out with Boffo on a leash, obediently staying beside Shanna. It was the only time he ever saw the dog behave, which was a good thing, because the dog probably outweighed her.

Shanna smiled and handed him a glass of iced tea. "I had a feeling you'd be thirsty."

He accepted it with a smile. "You're right; I am thirsty. Thank you, Mrs. McPherson."

She smiled back. "You're welcome, Mr. Gafferty. We'll be back in about fifteen minutes with Matthew."

Brendan rested one fist on his hip and watched them until they disappeared around the corner of the house, headed in the direction of the school.

With any new job, Brendan always initially addressed clients by their last name; because, after all, this was business. However, his clients always insisted that things be more casual and that they talk with Brendan on a first-name basis.

Shanna McPherson was the only one who didn't. It unnerved him, maybe because it had never happened to him before, especially with a woman, married or single. He didn't like the formality, which was another reason he would be glad when this job was over and he could move on to his next contract.

As happened every day, Shanna, her children, and her dog returned right on schedule. As usual, Shanna tried to coax the kids to go into the house, and they weren't cooperating.

"It's okay, Mrs. McPherson. I can give them something to do. I don't mind."

Her expression was a mixture of a question and relief, which made the extra work worthwhile.

The second she went inside, Brendan handed a small bag to Ashley. "I need you to go pick the weeds out from underneath the fence over there."

Ashley didn't move. She just looked up at him, her brown eyes big and wide, exactly like her mother's.

He looked down. All of Ashley's features were a very

close resemblance—like looking at Shanna in miniature form. It made him wonder what Shanna was like as a girl, then older, before the weight of all the responsibility settled onto her shoulders. He had to guess that Shanna was probably about the same age as himself, in her late twenties, even though signs of stress were already starting to show in a face that was much too young for such things. It made him wonder if there was anything he could do about it, besides fixing up her yard.

The thought startled Brendan. He shouldn't have been thinking about Shanna's history or her troubles.

He cleared his throat. "Yes, Ashley?"

She continued to look up, and he couldn't look away. The first thought that crossed his mind was that since Shanna needed more money, she should sign Ashley up for television commercials. Maybe even Shanna herself, too. Shanna wasn't exactly movie-star beautiful, but she was pretty and had a wholesome, honest face. He wondered if it was hard for adults to break into being photographed for magazine ads. He would certainly be drawn to an ad with a photo of Shanna featuring a product, especially if it had anything to do with gardening.

"What does a weed look like?"

Brendan gathered his thoughts. "If it's not grass, it's a weed, Ashley. I need everything that isn't grass pulled out so we can put the new grass on top."

Ashley nodded and walked across the yard to begin her appointed task.

Brendan handed Matthew his smallest shovel. "And you, young man, would you like to fill in the hole Boffo made?" He pointed to the dog's handiwork.

The boy didn't move.

Matthew looked up at him. His eyes were green, different than his mother's. Brendan could see some of Shanna's features in the boy, but also some that obviously came from his father, which made him wonder what Matthew's father was like.

Brendan gritted his teeth. The children's parentage was of no concern to him.

"Do you have a question, Matthew?"

"Will fixing up the yard make my mom happy?"

"I suppose so. That's why I'm here."

"What if it doesn't? I saw on TV that ladies get happy when they go out on a date. I want my mom to be happy. Can you tell me how to take her on a date?"

Brendan's mind went blank for a second. "How old are you, Matthew?"

Matthew stiffened to his full height, which in Brendan's opinion, wasn't much. "Six. But I'm almost seven."

Brendan lowered himself until one knee touched the ground, hoping it would make their conversation feel more man-to-man. "I have an idea. I think your mom needs to go on a date with a grown-up. I know your church is really small, but my church is really big. We have a group of men and women about the same age as your mom who do things together. Would you like me to ask your mom if she wants to go there, and maybe one of the other grown-ups will ask her on a date?"

Brendan didn't attend the singles' group, but he knew many single mothers who were regular participants. He wasn't personally interested in Shanna, but as long as it was clear it wasn't a date, Brendan wouldn't mind taking Shanna and introducing her around. He could even consider it an outreach ministry.

Not that he was closed off to the idea of dating—he actually looked forward to settling down and getting married one day. But when that day came, he wasn't going to hook up with a single mother. Yes, he wanted children—he already had plans for his children. He'd carefully calculated that, at his present income level, he could raise two children to have the college education he had been denied. If he could only do it for two, then those two children were going to be from his own genetic pool, not another man's children.

Some might have thought him shallow for thinking that way, but he knew what it was like to spread an income too thin. After his father died, even though his mother had tried hard to hide it, he'd seen how she struggled to make ends meet. Even though he'd been much too young, he'd helped earn the money needed for his family to pay the bills, even if it was only a family of two. He didn't want his children to face those same struggles and insecurities about not having enough money. His children would have all they needed, including the college education he didn't have. And that meant exactly two.

Matthew nodded. "Yes. I would like it if you took my mom to that place."

Brendan stood. "Okay, Matthew, that's settled. Now it's time to get back to work."

two

Shanna's heart pumped with excitement. The work on her yard wasn't nearly completed, but already she'd received a result from one of her queries. "Yes, I'm still taking new clients," she said to the man on the phone.

She could hear the smile in the man's voice. "Good. I've checked your references and gone over what you sent me. What you're offering looks exactly like what I need. I know it's short notice, but can we set up a meeting at your office in about an hour or so?"

The excitement turned into a lump of cardboard in her stomach. She needed the deposit on this contract or she couldn't make her next mortgage payment. But she couldn't afford for this new potential client to see the mess, or the same thing would happen as when the last potential clients went through.

Shanna stiffened in her chair. "I'm going to be honest with you, Bill. I'm in the middle of renovation to my office, which is in my home. The work on my office is complete, so it has a separate entrance from my residence, but I still have someone working on the outside. Things are still noisy and a bit distracting out there."

She watched as Matthew threw Boffo's ball into the air, then whacked it with the small shovel like a baseball bat, sending the ball flying across the yard with Boffo in pursuit.

"I wondered about that, from your address. That's

interesting. I also run my business out of my home. I started it with just me and my wife, and then we renovated, like you, so it was set apart from the rest of the house. We felt it was important to separate it at that point. Since then, we've grown so much that we've got ten employees now. We've expanded again and now need a real accountant instead of my wife doing the bookkeeping. She can't keep up, and she doesn't know how to do all the new government stuff. Also, since we incorporated, we need an accountant to do our corporate income tax returns."

"That's what I do. Perhaps I could come down to your office?" If she could find a sitter.

Shanna glanced into the backyard, where Brendan was lining up some bricks in the back corner. Since he'd started working for her, both Matthew and Ashley spent most of their time outside with him. Shanna was almost sure he wouldn't mind if she had to run out for a few hours, although to leave him in charge of the children in her absence surely made him the highest-priced babysitter in Seattle. It wasn't something she wanted to do, but she didn't have any other options on short notice.

"I don't think that will be necessary. You were highly recommended, and hearing that you've invested in your office the same way I did tells me that you plan to be around for a long time. How about if you e-mail me your rates and a proposal, and that will probably be enough to get started."

"That would be great," she said, trying to make it sound like she made this kind of agreement all the time. She was so excited she could barely keep from shouting for joy. The last few weeks she'd been so discouraged that she'd begun to wonder if she'd made a mistake—that Brendan's work, and her investment, weren't going to make a difference. Instead, God's timing was perfect, and for the first time in a long time, she felt encouraged.

Shanna picked up a pen and paper. "Just let me write down your e-mail address, and I can have something prepared for you by the end of the day. When can you send your deposit?"

She held her breath. The cost to renovate the office to include installing the outside door had been more expensive than the estimate. But she couldn't leave the project half finished or it meant nothing. In faith, she'd contracted Brendan's services to do the yard when she really didn't have the money. Pastor Harry had told her that she needed to trust in God, and that was exactly what she was doing.

Of course, it helped that Pastor Harry had promised that Brendan's work was excellent, and his rates were more than reasonable.

"I just need a day to go over your proposal, but I'm pretty sure everything will be fine. Good day, Shanna."

Shanna hung up the phone, barely able to restrain a squeal of excitement.

This was it—her largest corporate client so far. The kind she needed to make a success of her business and support her family without having to worry about where the next penny was coming from.

But before she could finish the proposal, she had a three o'clock deadline for another client's project that she had to complete first. It wasn't ethical to break a promise, no matter how important this was.

Shanna started to press the key to complete her current

reconciliation when Ashley's shriek sliced through the air.

Shanna fumbled her transaction on the keyboard.

She scrambled to her feet and leaned as far over her desk as she could, frantically searching out the window to see what was wrong.

In the back of the yard, beside what was left of Shanna's fence, Ashley stood, pointing with her entire arm extended, screaming words that Shanna couldn't understand. As Ashley's arm moved, her gaze followed a moving target that Shanna couldn't see.

Not far from Ashley, in the corner, Matthew stood facing the same moving target, his shovel frozen in midair. His mouth hung wide open, just like a character in a bad cartoon.

Shanna pressed her palms to the window, leaning so close that the tip of her nose brushed the cool glass.

Suddenly, a blur of red plaid and faded blue flashed past the window.

Shanna lurched backward. Before she could catch herself, she tripped on the wheeled leg of her office chair. She felt herself falling backward, but instead of landing on the hard floor, she fell into the seat and rolled backward a few inches.

Not caring that she would knock over her client's papers, Shanna launched herself out of the chair and scrambled up onto the desktop on her hands and knees to watch yet another fiasco unfurling.

This time, something green and pink hung from Boffo's mouth as Brendan chased Boffo in a circle around the backyard. Still in the corner, Matthew snapped his mouth shut and threw down the shovel. He ran into Boffo's path, extending his arms fully on both sides to block the dog.

Boffo could have dodged the child, with or without Brendan closing in from behind. Instead, Boffo dropped his prize at Matthew's feet.

His chest heaving, Brendan skidded to a halt behind the dog, nearly falling in the loose dirt. All was silent as he stared down at the soggy green and pink lump at Boffo's feet. Shanna recognized it as one of the miniature carnations Brendan had given Matthew to plant in the flower bed under construction in the corner of the backyard.

Brendan squatted to scoop up the bedraggled plant, saying something she couldn't hear to the dog as he picked it up. In response, Boffo lunged forward, thrusting his large, muddy paws onto Brendan's shoulders.

Brendan tumbled backward. His arms flailed, but he couldn't regain his balance with Boffo's weight pressing into him. Brendan's legs shot out from under him, and down he went, along with Boffo. The plant flew up out of his hand and landed on Matthew's head at the same time Brendan's back thumped to the ground. He exhaled with an "oof" as Boffo bounced on his chest.

Brendan struggled for breath with the huge dog sprawled on top of him. Brendan was trapped. Nothing would move Boffo if Boffo didn't want to be moved.

Ashley squealed with glee, then giggled. The shrill sound prompted Boffo into high gear. His tongue flashed out toward Brendan's face.

"No!" Brendan gasped, calling out as he raised his arms, but he was too late to protect himself from the onslaught of Boffo's sloppy doggy kisses.

Ashley appeared beside them. "Him loves you!" she sang

as she danced in a circle, waving her arms above her head and spinning around on her toes.

Still atop the desk, with her elbows fixed on the hard surface, Shanna leaned forward and buried her face in her palms.

The man was never going to get her landscaping done. Either that or he was going to quit, and it would be all her fault.

She didn't want him to leave. Not just for the job he was doing, and not for herself. Despite the havoc, her children hadn't had such fun with a man since. . .Shanna couldn't remember.

An ache formed in the depths of her soul. When their father was alive, the children hadn't had as much fun with him as they did with this patient stranger. Roger had refused to have anything to do with his children— something Shanna hadn't seen coming in their marriage. Roger had promised that he'd wanted to have children, yet he'd probably changed only one diaper in all the time he was a father. That was when Shanna had the flu and had locked herself in the bathroom, throwing up. Roger never played with the children, claiming he didn't know what to do with them. Actually, Roger simply couldn't be bothered. He made no effort to hide it when either she or the children annoyed him, which was most of the time.

Brendan Gafferty, a stranger, had spent more time with Matthew and Ashley in the last week than their father had in the whole year prior to his death. He was also being a good sport about their antics and Boffo's behavior, something Roger never would have been.

However, as beneficial as it was for her children to have a

good relationship with a male figure, she couldn't allow the hired help to do anything more than the job he was hired for. There was still too much to do. She didn't know if it was just luck or the grace of God that she got a new client before everything was finished. She certainly wouldn't test God to provide more before everything was ready.

Shanna slowly lowered her feet to the floor and walked outside. She couldn't afford the distraction, but she had to take Boffo and the children into the house and let Brendan get back to his work. Maybe, since the children had been so busy with him, they might go to bed early tonight. Then she could get some work done in peace and quiet and still get a few hours of sleep before she had to wake Matthew for school the next day.

By the time she reached them, Brendan had the situation back under control. Matthew recovered the plant Boffo had stolen and was diligently patting the dirt down around it, even though it looked rather bedraggled compared to the rest. Ashley sang to herself, completely off-key, as she picked rocks out of the mud and piled them into Brendan's wheelbarrow. Even Boffo was doing something constructive. Shanna didn't know how he did it, but somehow Brendan had manipulated the dog into digging a hole where she knew he planned to plant an apple tree when the other yard work was completed.

She cleared her throat to get everyone's attention. "Matthew, Ashley, how would you like to come into the house for some cookies and juice? Mr. Gafferty, could I offer you a cup of coffee?" Shanna knew she could certainly use a good cup of strong coffee. Maybe even a whole pot.

"Does we have to go into the house?" Ashley muttered.

"I was having fun helping Mr. Brendan."

"Coffee?" Brendan's eyebrows arched. "Uh. . . Actually, if you still have some of that iced tea you gave me earlier, that would be real nice of you."

"Certainly." Shanna reached down to take Ashley's hand. "Come on, Ashley. We have to let—" She stopped moving and looked up. *"Mr. Brendan?"*

Brendan shrugged his shoulders. "I'm not used to all this Mr. and Mrs. stuff all the time. But if that's what you want the kids to do, I'm okay with that. I just thought this would be a good compromise. Besides, my father was Mr. Gafferty. I'm just Brendan."

Shanna stared at him. Part of her reason for the way both she and the children addressed him was a sign of respect, because he deserved it. Brendan Gafferty was a hard worker and kept his word, unlike their father. But there was another reason she addressed him so formally. She wanted to keep a professional distance. She knew she should have trusted him; after all, he was a close friend of her pastor. Yet she didn't feel comfortable with him. If she kept their relationship formal, she felt safe. Being his employer—and only his employer—was the way to accomplish that.

However, she had to consider her children first. Brendan Gafferty was setting a good example for them, acting the way a good man should behave toward children, the way their father should have behaved.

She cleared her throat and stiffened her posture, but he still towered over her, negating her efforts to look like an authority figure. "Fine, then. Come on, Matthew, Ashley. We should let Mr. Brendan get back to his work. He has a lot to do. Boffo, come."

"You really don't have to take the kids; they were okay. Of course, I don't mind you taking the dog."

Shanna sighed. "I'm so sorry about Boffo. I know he's not very well behaved, but he's very friendly, and we love him a lot." He was also big. Even though he didn't have a vicious bone in his body, Boffo at least had the potential to look like a watchdog to those who didn't know him.

Ashley nodded so fast her bangs bounced on her forehead. "And him loves us lots, too."

Brendan crossed his arms over his chest. "I'm sure he does."

Shanna glanced back and forth between her children and the dog, then at her wristwatch. Maybe Boffo would sleep. . . .

She bent down to talk to the children at eye level. "Matthew, you can stay out here only if you promise to be good. But it's time for Ashley to have a nap. I think Boffo could use a nap, too. Ashley, you can come back out later, after you have a little rest." Shanna hoped this would give her enough time to accomplish something constructive.

Because of all the excitement, Ashley fell asleep quickly, and fortunately so did Boffo. Having him sleep beside Shanna's desk was perfect, because she knew where he was *and* what he was doing.

Shanna resumed her work.

Except she couldn't concentrate.

Pastor Harry had been right. Brendan was a good man and a hard worker. Without distraction, he accomplished a lot. He'd shown Matthew how to stuff dirt into the crevices in a pile of rocks that was to become a rock garden. At first, when he'd explained the cheapest way to cover the unsightly boulders that couldn't be moved, she'd had doubts. But now, as the pile was beginning to rise, she could see and appreciate the potential.

She continued to watch Brendan as he worked. He rammed a crowbar beneath a rock with such brute force, she flinched at the contact, even though he was across the yard and she was inside her office.

The phone rang. The caller ID showed her brother-in-law's number. Just seeing the number made her hand shake as she picked up the handset.

"We have to talk," Ray barked.

Her hand shook even worse.

She sucked in a deep breath and stiffened, trying to give herself strength through an unrelenting posture. "I told you not to use my business number."

"I want you to come here tomorrow."

She gritted her teeth. "No. I have work to do. Besides, we have nothing to talk about. I told you that before. Leave me alone."

The bang of Ray slamming the phone down echoed in her ear.

Shanna slouched and squeezed her eyes shut. She didn't want to deal with Ray in person. It was bad enough over the phone, with the safety of the distance between them. Her life was hard enough with the everyday struggles of trying to earn enough money to pay the bills while looking after Ashley and Matthew. With the added problems between the landscaper and her dog, she couldn't handle anything more right now.

"Excuse me? Shanna?"

Shanna opened her eyes and straightened in the chair,

quickly dropping her hands into her lap and twining her fingers together tightly.

Brendan stood in the doorway. At the sound of his arrival, Boffo stood and sprinted the few yards to close the distance, then sat in front of Brendan, his unruly tail swooshing on the ground while he looked up.

Brendan reached forward and gave the dog a short pat, then tilted his head and narrowed his eyes slightly as he looked at Shanna. "Is something wrong?"

"It's nothing." And it would stay nothing, because she refused to go to her brother-in-law's house. She wasn't going to get involved in another confrontation. Her number one priority was her children, not trying to placate Ray. "Is there something you need?"

"I'm going to have Matthew water down the mud in the rocks, but he says he doesn't know where his rubber boots are kept."

Shanna felt her cheeks turn warm. "That's because he doesn't have rubber boots. He only has one pair of boots— winter boots—if they still fit. I hate buying boots for the kids when they grow out of them in a year. I never know if it's going to snow from one winter to the next. You know this Seattle weather."

Brendan nodded. "Yes. When I was growing up, most years my mother didn't buy me boots for exactly those reasons. I did just fine, going to school in my sneakers. All of my friends did that when we were kids." He paused and smiled broadly. "In fact, I remember when we all thought we were way too cool to wear boots. But on this job, good rubber boots are a must."

Shanna nodded. As an accountant, she didn't need rubber

boots, although she did own one pair of good leather boots. But like Brendan, she remembered many years as a child when she didn't have winter boots because it generally didn't get too cold most winters along the coast in Washington State. Thinking of weather, she wondered what landscapers did when the growing season was over. Seattle didn't get snow most winters, but it was still cold enough not to want to work outside.

Shanna mentally shook her head to clear her thoughts. What he did in his off-seasons was none of her business. He was there to transform her lot of mismatched grass and stray boulders into a presentable and professionally landscaped yard, which hopefully wouldn't take too much longer. Then Brendan and his rubber boots would be long gone.

She looked up to see him checking out her desk. He'd been working for her for a week, and this was the first time he'd been inside.

"So this is where you run your accounting business," he said. "Harry told me about how you're trying to expand."

She nodded. "I'm already doing bookkeeping for a few home-based businesses, but I need some larger corporate clients."

Brendan glanced at a stack of files on top of one of the cabinets. "Does that bookkeeping for home-based businesses include self-employed individuals?"

"Yes. That's what most home-based businesses are."

"Does your work include preparing self-employed income tax returns?"

"It sure does."

"I've been really busy, and I just got a second notice to file taxes from the year before last. If you've got the time, maybe we could make a deal. If you could get my taxes done before I have to pay a penalty, I could do something extra for you. Your kids are pretty active. How about if I build them a playscape in the yard here, where you can keep an eye on them? I can build it so it looks like one you see in a playground, not one of those typical backyard types."

Shanna gasped. "I can't afford that!" She could barely make ends meet as it was. But a good play center would be the perfect solution. It would keep Matthew and Ashley from being bored, especially since soon Matthew would be out of school for the summer. And if it was set in the right location, she could watch the children playing without leaving her desk.

"Maybe you didn't understand what I was saying. I didn't mean for you to pay for it. I could build it for you and provide the materials. After all, I get everything whole-sale. I'll even do it to match the fence. After I fix the fence, of course. That would be in exchange for doing my bookkeeping."

Shanna narrowed her eyes. "That's a very large project. Just exactly how do you do your bookkeeping if you think this is going to be an even exchange?"

His ears reddened. "Usually I file late when I get caught up in the winter, but this year I took on a few additional contract projects for the municipality, and I didn't have any spare time. And then the new landscaping season started early, and, well. . .I never did get a chance to catch up."

"Exactly how far behind are you?"

The shade of his ears deepened. "I'm usually pretty good about entering everything into my program; I just have a hard time balancing it. But since last April, I've kind of been throwing everything in a box. Well, actually two boxes. And I just started a third one."

"April? This is nearly the end of June. You're not talking months; you're talking two years of back taxes, plus whatever has transpired this fiscal year, aren't you?"

"Uh. . .yeah."

From his sudden silence, Shanna had the feeling they weren't talking about mere shoe-box-sized boxes—despite the size of his feet, which looked to be about a size 13, to support his height. "What kind of boxes are we dealing with?"

"The kind I get from my supplier where I order my gardening stuff."

Her head spun at the potential volume.

Yet Brendan's offer would provide the perfect solution to watch her children in the yard while she worked. This way, they wouldn't beg her to take them to the park, where there was no computer.

"I think you've got yourself a deal."

three

Brendan stepped back to survey his handiwork.

Phase one was nearly done. The boulders were in place for the two rockeries, and everything else had been cleared out. The top layer of soil had been picked clean of smaller rocks, and he had rototilled in a good base of topsoil and peat.

Now he was ready to lay the sod. Originally Shanna had requested that he seed the lawn because it was cheaper, but since she was going to do two and a half years of his bookkeeping and file his tax returns, he didn't want to do "cheap." Within an hour, a truck was scheduled to come with the sod he'd ordered, and by suppertime that day, she'd have an instant lawn.

It was a pity that now her front yard wasn't going to look as good as the back. It was something he'd take care of later. He had a feeling she was going to deserve it, and more.

For the past week, he'd barely seen Shanna. However, he'd seen a lot of her dog. While she'd buried herself in his paperwork in her home office, her dog had buried most of his tools in her backyard. Fortunately for him, her children thought it was a bigger game than the dog did. They pretended they were secret spies, hiding behind the rockeries, watching every time Boffo buried his treasure of the moment. Then, when Boffo moved on to his next conquest and was digging a new hole in the fresh dirt across the yard, they would go to where he'd just been and unbury the last thing that had disappeared just when Brendan needed it.

It wasn't the ideal way to finish a project, but it kept everyone busy. If he had to look on the bright side, even though it had cost him a couple of extra-small shovels, the children were quite happy to help. They'd almost finished picking up all the loose stones and loading them into the wheelbarrow, which saved him a lot of bending. Since they were having fun, he didn't think he was contravening any child-labor laws by having the children pick up rocks for him. As a reward, he'd treated them at the ice-cream truck a few times, but only when Shanna wasn't watching; because he knew she'd tell him that the ice-cream truck was too expensive.

Again, he surveyed the yard. It had been two long weeks, but everything was perfect and ready for the next step.

A noisy vehicle approached on the street, echoing sounds of a motor that needed more than just a good tune-up. At the sound of it stopping in front of the house, Boffo went stiff. He laid his ears back, his lips curled to show huge, white teeth, and a low growl rolled from his throat.

The hairs on the back of Brendan's neck prickled. For as long as he'd been here, and after all of his scuffles with the dog, not once had he ever heard the dog growl. Not including closed doors and the chain used to tie him up, the only thing Boffo barked at was the neighborhood squirrel.

"Stay here, Boffo. I have to see what's out there." He paused for just a second, wondering why he was talking to Shanna's dog, then made his way to the front.

Of course Boffo didn't stay. Brendan shoved the dog back and kept him at bay with one arm while he squeezed through the gate, then made sure it was firmly closed behind him. He walked quickly to the front of the house, ignoring Boffo jumping and throwing his weight against the gate that held him back.

Just as Brendan stepped from between Shanna's house and her neighbor's, a scruffy man knocked on Shanna's front door.

The door opened.

"Ray? What are you doing here?"

"I came to talk."

"We have nothing to talk about."

"Maybe you didn't hear me. I said I came to talk." Despite Shanna's protest, Ray barged inside.

Brendan ran the rest of the way. Before the door closed in his face, he raised one hand to block it and stepped inside.

Shanna's foyer was large enough to accommodate four or five people without anyone having to go up the stairs. Yet despite there being so much room, Ray moved much too close to Shanna, forcing her to back up until she was against the wall. When she had nowhere to go, Ray edged to the side to block any means of escape, either up the stairs or past him through the door.

All the color drained from Shanna's face until she was as white as bonemeal.

Brendan quickly stepped behind Ray just as Ray opened his mouth.

"Excuse me," Brendan said, before Ray could speak. "Do you need something?"

Ray spun around to face him, then backed up one step,

which gave Shanna a little breathing room.

Ray's eyes narrowed. "Who are you?" he ground out from between clenched teeth.

"The name's Gafferty. Brendan Gafferty." Brendan straightened himself to his full height of six feet five inches, deliberately towering well above Ray, who was a "short" guy at only six feet tall. Brendan normally didn't like to intimidate people with his size and height, but today he used his stature to his advantage. He lowered his voice, then stepped between Ray and Shanna. "I don't believe you were invited."

Ray glanced up at Brendan, then glared at Shanna. "I'll be back," he snapped. "This isn't finished." Without saying *what* wasn't finished, he stomped out of the house to his pickup. It started reluctantly with a puff of blue smoke, then roared away, rubber squealing, leaving dark marks on the road in its wake.

Shanna pressed herself into the wall behind her. "You have good timing," she mumbled. "Thank you."

"It wasn't really timing. Boffo started acting funny, so I came to check out what was upsetting him. Who was that?"

"He's my husband's brother."

"The one who has the dog you think would hurt Boffo?"

"Yes."

Brendan turned his head in the direction Ray's truck had disappeared. From the looks of Ray, Ray could hurt Boffo without help from his evil dog.

He turned back to Shanna, who was still pressed against the wall. Most of the color had returned to her face, although she still didn't look very good.

"Why are you so afraid of him? What has he done?"

"I—I," she stammered, "don't trust him."

He could see why. Brendan wouldn't trust him, either, and he'd only seen Ray for a few moments. "It's okay. He's gone now."

Shanna stepped away from the wall, but only a few inches. "Yes. Which means I should get back to work."

Brendan watched as Shanna brushed some imaginary dirt off her sleeves while she composed herself. Something inside his stomach felt funny, but he didn't think he was hungry.

He didn't know if he felt more angry or sickened by Ray's behavior. He'd seen bullies in school, and such behavior made him angry back then. His mother had been called to the school many times to talk to the principal after he'd been in a fight—not that Brendan had actually been involved in any fights. Knowing no one could beat him, he always broke up fights between a bully and his smaller victims. In the process, though, he often took a few hits and gave a few back.

But this was different than anything he'd ever experienced. Even though he'd stopped a few fights as an adult, he'd never stepped between a man and a woman.

Ray was trouble looking for a place to happen.

Even outside of his circle of Christian friends, he'd never been in a situation where he thought a man was about to hit a woman. Ray hadn't actually raised his fists, yet the air was thick with intimidation and Shanna's fear. It made him uneasy that even though Ray was gone for now, judging from Shanna's reaction, what happened wasn't new or entirely unexpected. He didn't want to think that

Ray would be back when Brendan wouldn't be here to interrupt.

The knowledge didn't sit well with him. Brendan wanted to know what Ray had wanted, but it wasn't his place to ask. He didn't really know Shanna that well. Their only association was the work they were doing for each other, and no more.

"The truck should be here with your new lawn anytime now. I need you to keep the kids in the house. And Boffo. Especially Boffo."

"Of course."

He waited for her to say something else, but she didn't. All he could hear was Boffo whining at the gate.

Brendan ran his fingers through his hair, then absently stroked his beard. "I have a few things to do before the truck comes, so I'd really appreciate it if you could get Boffo out of the yard. If he buries any more of my tools and I don't notice before we start putting the sod down, they'll be gone forever."

"Of course." She started to turn toward the doorway to go through the house to the back, but Brendan turned toward the front.

"I'll go back out the way I came rather than tracking mud through your house."

"Oh. Thank you."

He stepped out, and the door closed behind him.

The lock clicked closed. A strange feeling of separation poked at him, which didn't make sense. Instead of returning to the backyard, Brendan stood facing the door, reminding himself that Shanna's problems with Ray weren't his concern. His only concern was to finish Shanna's landscaping.

As he stood staring blankly at the wooden surface, a huge *whump* banged at the door from inside, so strong that it shook from the impact. Brendan stepped back in an automatic reaction, then smiled. Boffo was most definitely inside.

Brendan returned to the backyard knowing that for once, he could open the gate without any 140-pound hairy surprises lurking, waiting for him on the other side.

He scanned the yard, looking for any lumps or bumps in his perfectly flat work. Sure enough, he did see a disturbance in all the work he'd done leveling the surface for the sod. Again, Boffo had struck.

Brendan gritted his teeth as he brushed the dirt away and pulled one of his good leather gloves to the surface. He stomped to the corner where he'd stacked his tools pending the arrival of the sod, retrieved a shovel, and leveled yet another piece of Boffo's handiwork.

In all the landscaping jobs he'd done, he'd never had a problem like this before. Yet he couldn't say Boffo was all bad. It had been fun to prepare the hole for the apple tree that would soon go into the corner of the yard, and it had been done faster than if he'd had to do all the digging alone. Once he showed Boffo where to dig, Boffo was anxious to please. Boffo's problem wasn't lack of understanding; it was lack of focus. Shanna simply didn't have the time to train the dog to live up to his potential.

The thought stopped him in his tracks. Boffo was a smart dog, even though he was horrendously undisciplined and as big as a small bear. Before he could spend any more time thinking about it, the sod truck lumbered up to the front of the house.

Brendan waved to Thomas, the driver. They'd been friends for years, ever since elementary school. Thomas waved back and began the process of lowering the miniature forklift down from its perch on the back of the flatbed to begin unloading the sod.

Brendan rolled up his sleeves.

He wasn't going to stress any more about Shanna's goofy dog. He had work to do.

&

Shanna tried her best to concentrate on her work, but she couldn't. With every trip the two men took carrying the rolls between the truck in the front and the backyard, Boffo ran back and forth, no doubt hoping that, by some miracle, a door would open somewhere and he could join them.

Shanna sighed. At least he would sleep well tonight.

Again, she tried to concentrate on balancing Brendan's expenses versus his credits. Ashley was down for her nap, and Matthew was in his room building what he claimed was going to be a cargo jet plane out of plastic bricks. She couldn't let the dog distract her when both of the children were quiet at the same time.

While she sorted through a pile of Brendan's receipts from a year and a half ago, the sound of his voice drifted into the house. She stopped working and watched the two men through the window. The task of leveling the yard was monumental, yet he'd done it in two weeks, cheerfully, despite the trials and tribulations of her children and her dog. He laid a section of sod down, positioned it to lie even with the piece beside it, rolled it out, then nudged it into place with his foot before he left to get another section.

Once, she'd helped a friend lay sod in the front yard. She'd barely been able to lift the heavy rolls of grass and mud, yet Brendan carried them effortlessly, sometimes two at a time. It shouldn't have been a surprise. She'd also watched him heave some of the boulders he'd dug up. She struggled to carry a bag of flour up the stairs and into the kitchen. She couldn't imagine carrying a boulder. Yet he did.

His strength was amazing. She could certainly understand why Ray had cowered in front of him.

She couldn't help her self-satisfied grin at the memory. She hoped Ray had felt a churning in his stomach and a pounding of his heart, knowing that he was no match for someone who finally stood up to him. Ray had lost this battle without a confrontation—and he'd left without what he came for. Shanna hoped Ray would remember that sensation of powerlessness and what it felt like to be on the other side of such treatment, and never forget it.

So far, Ray hadn't hit her, but often she'd felt it was close. Only the grace of God had saved her—by either a distraction or unexpected witnesses.

Roger had been the same way; only being married to him, there was nowhere to hide. When Roger couldn't get his way by screaming at her, he resorted to violence, some days worse than others. It hadn't happened often, compared to some of the relationships she'd learned about, but even once was too much.

Her own father had treated her mother that way. Shanna recognized the signs, but once married to Roger, she didn't know how to break the cycle of spousal abuse. Sometimes she could calm Roger when he lost his temper, but not always. When they first got married, she'd admired his strength and power, but it hadn't taken long before things began to change. When they started their family, it had been a mutual decision for her to give up her career and stay home to raise their children while Roger went out to work to support the family, including her. However, the warm fuzzies hadn't lasted long, if they'd ever happened at all. Roger's resentment of being forced to work and be the only income earner grew almost daily, especially after Matthew was born. When she became pregnant with Ashley, things became so bad that she thought she was reliving the life of her mother. The strength that had initially attracted her to Roger had become what drove them apart.

By the time she realized she'd been caught in the downward spiral, Ashley was born. With a new baby and a toddler, she felt trapped in a prison of her own making. None of her friends believed her when she told them what Roger was like hidden behind the walls of their home. Just as no one had believed her mother, either. It was only the love of Jesus that held Shanna together.

When Roger was killed in a car accident, rather than fighting grief, she'd fought guilt—guilt because she was free of the horrible way he'd treated her. It had also spared her from making a painful decision. The night before he died, Roger told her that he wanted a divorce because he'd found another woman. Her pride had been hurt, but by then she didn't love him anymore—she'd been afraid of him for too long. Still, she wanted to do the right thing. She'd been willing to attend counseling sessions to work it out. After all, she'd loved him once. But she didn't get the chance. Less than twelve hours later, Roger was dead.

Shanna knew she might want to get married again.

But when that happened, she would marry someone like herself—a nice, nearsighted, deskbound accountant, whose favorite pastime was sitting at his computer playing online games. A nerd. A man who was masculine but could be comfortable with his tender, feminine side—a man who would treat her gently and speak quietly. Someone who would confer with her and discuss issues. Someone who wouldn't take over and do everything his own way, claiming he knew what was best, then become angry when she had the nerve to disagree. She needed to be an equal participant in a relationship.

Male voices echoed from the backyard. Shanna refocused her thoughts and looked outside at Brendan and the other man. From the way the two men spoke, it was obvious they were friends, yet nothing distracted them from their work. Not much time had elapsed, and only a small section remained uncovered. Brendan and his friend were now carrying the last pieces into the yard. His friend carried one roll, and Brendan carried two.

Brendan's friend stood to the side while Brendan pulled a knife from his belt and began to cut those final pieces into shape. He tucked them into place, then nudged the last piece with his foot. They were done.

She stared, not able to tear her eyes away as Brendan stretched, then rubbed his biceps. His muscles bulged as he flexed his arms. She didn't remember such muscles on Paul Bunyan.

The mental picture of how Brendan had come between her and Ray flashed through her mind. If she had any doubt then, she had no doubt now. If he wanted to, Brendan could have squashed Ray like a bug.

Boffo came to her and raised one paw to rest on her leg as she sat in her chair. She turned the chair and leaned to wrap her arms around him, needing to feel his size and strength. She wasn't entirely sure, because she'd gotten Boffo after Roger died; but she hoped that if someone came at her, even someone he saw often, Boffo would protect her.

The two men walked to the front of the yard for the last time. Within minutes the truck rumbled to a start and drove away. Not long after that, Brendan appeared inside her office.

"We're done. I'm going to call it quits for the day as soon as I get the sprinkler going. Can you make sure the kids don't go on the grass tonight?"

"What about Boffo? It's going to be hard to keep him out of his own backyard all night."

He reached to the wall and pulled Boffo's leash off the hook where it hung by the door. "You don't have to worry about Boffo. I have plans for both of us. Tonight Boffo and I are going to dog school."

The second Boffo noticed that Brendan had his leash, the traitor surged out of Shanna's grip and bounded to Brendan. He alternately circled Brendan's feet and jumped up for the leash so fast that his feet skidded on the linoleum and he almost fell.

Shanna ignored Boffo and stared up at Brendan. "Excuse me?"

"Boffo's not really a bad dog," he said as he raised the leash over his head, causing Boffo to miss it as he once again leaped for it. "He just needs a firm hand and a little training. I was talking to a friend, and I enrolled Boffo in his dog obedience class that starts tonight."

"Obedience class?"

Brendan nodded, then switched hands, breaking Boffo's rhythm as the dog continued to attempt to gain possession of his leash. Brendan kept talking, with Boffo scrambling and jumping around him as if the dog were nothing more than an annoying fly. "Jeff owes me a favor. He had an opening that would have gone empty, so he let me in for free as long as I promised to spread the word for anyone else who wants to enroll next session. Rather than bringing Boffo back late at night, I figured he could spend the night at my place. I'll just bring him back in the morning when I come back to work. I don't think my neighbors would mind."

Finished with his explanation, Brendan reached down, snagged Boffo by the collar, and pushed him down. Through a battle of intense physical strength, he forced the hyper dog into a sitting position. Despite Boffo's struggles, Brendan never lost his grip. When Boffo was finally convinced that he was overpowered, he stopped struggling.

Once Boffo was completely motionless, Brendan released Boffo's collar and scratched him behind the ears. "That won't happen again, dog. Mark my words," Brendan muttered. "Next time, you're going to behave."

Shanna gritted her teeth. Her automatic reaction was to cower and mutter an agreement that what he was doing was the best thing. But even if it was the best thing, he hadn't discussed it with her first. And that was exactly the opposite of what she told herself would happen after Roger died. It was time to take control of her life and direct the things that happened around her, including her wayward dog.

She summoned all her courage and stood straight, stretching to make herself as tall as possible. "I would have appreciated it if you'd asked me first."

He stared down at the ground, avoiding eye contact. "I didn't want you to insist on paying for it. I want you to consider this paying back a favor."

"We don't owe each other any favors. We're exchanging a business deal."

He raised his head and looked into her eyes. "To tell the truth, I was thinking that you're probably going to be doing a lot more extra hours on my bookkeeping than I'll be doing in your yard."

"But there's the added expense of the materials for the playscape to take into account."

"I know the price my friends pay their accountants to do taxes. That cost alone, without the other stuff you have to do to get to that point, is already way more than what I'm going to spend on the materials. Remember, I'm paying wholesale."

"But the cost of your labor per hour has to be taken into account, too."

"Those things are pretty easy to put together, actually. They come with instructions."

"Instructions?"

"Yeah. Instructions. I may be a male, but I do read instructions."

She felt her mouth drop open.

"You know. When you buy something that's not assembled, there's this book that comes with it. It tells you how to put it together. There's even pictures."

"Pictures?"

"It shows you how to put piece A into slot B and fasten with bolt C."

She stared at him, not knowing what to say and trying to remember how the conversation started. "What does this have to do with Boffo, again?"

He sighed. "I wanted to even up the deal, so I got him into dog school. It won't teach him how to be a watchdog, but he'll be easier to live with, and people will look at him differently when he listens to what you say."

Shanna stared at Brendan as she mentally sorted his words. The main reason she'd brought Boffo home from the animal shelter was because he looked like a watchdog, even if he didn't act like one. Everyone quickly found out that Boffo was a lover, not a fighter. But now things had changed. It wasn't strangers she needed protection from— it was her brother-in-law. If she understood Brendan's unstated message, Ray was more likely to keep his distance if he thought Boffo might actually obey a command to do something to protect her. Then dog school would be worth it, and then some.

"All right. But I'm going to keep track of my hours, and I want you to keep track of your hours and expenses." She didn't want to owe anyone—including her landscaper— anything.

"Deal. Now if you'll excuse me, I don't want to be late."

Before she could respond or reconsider, he turned and left with Boffo straining and pulling on the leash so hard that Brendan had to lean slightly backward to brace himself to maintain his balance.

When man and dog rounded the corner, Shanna ran to the front of the house to watch through the blinds. As soon as they reached Brendan's pickup and Brendan opened the door, Boffo changed his mind, digging his feet into the ground. But by the time he started to turn and try to run the other way, Brendan had grabbed him in such a way that he couldn't escape. With an extreme amount of effort and maneuvering of the flailing dog, Brendan shoved him up onto the seat, then slammed the door.

As Brendan drove away, Boffo jumped and clawed at the back window, just as he did when she took him to the vet.

"Good luck," she whispered, not sure if she was talking to Brendan or the dog.

four

As promised, Brendan arrived right on time in the morning with Boffo in tow. Or was it himself that was in tow? He hadn't quite figured that out.

He'd expected most of the dogs to behave badly at dog school last night. He just hadn't expected to be the one with the worst-case scenario. His friend Jeff had used Boffo's behavior as the bad example of what the other class participants were to avoid.

The gate had barely closed behind him when Shanna's office door opened. Immediately, the movement caught Boffo's eye. The dog lunged forward with all his strength. Since Brendan hadn't expected the dog to bolt inside his own yard, the leash slipped out of his hand.

Fear clenched his gut. "Shanna!" he shouted, then started running, despite knowing he would never be able to catch Boffo. The image of Boffo jumping on her and slamming her into the metal frame of the doorway pierced through his mind. He now knew exactly how much the dog weighed and the result of being slammed with that weight, because he'd experienced it the hard way.

"Brace yourself!" Brendan shouted as he ran faster. "Boffo—"

Before he could finish yelling out his warning, Shanna dropped to her hands and knees. Boffo skidded to a halt in front of her and frantically began licking her face and dancing, his tail wagging so fast it was a blur. Shanna threw her arms around the dog, balanced herself on her knees, tilted her head back, and laughed.

"Yes! I missed you, too!" She giggled as Boffo sloppily licked her cheeks. Behind her, Ashley appeared in the doorway. At the sight of her mother and Boffo, Ashley called out Boffo's name and clapped her hands.

Brendan stopped short, feeling like an idiot. He should have known that Shanna knew what to expect and what to do so that she wouldn't get plowed down as he had. She was a smart woman.

He smiled at the whole happily-ever-after scene. A happy mom, a happy daughter, and an overly happy dog. He wished he were a part of it instead of an outsider looking in.

His smile faded. Being a part of this scene wasn't part of his plan. He was only working here. Shanna didn't want him involved in her personal affairs; she'd made that point more than clear. Everything she said and did indicated that this was supposed to be business only, which was how he wanted it, too. Yet he liked Shanna. She was resourceful, determined, loyal, an excellent parent, and a hard worker. In a few short weeks, he'd also come to like her kids. If he were forced to admit it, he would have to say that he was even getting attached to her nutty dog.

Normally a job was a job, but this time he knew that when this job was over, he would be asking Harry for updates on Shanna and her little family. He'd even been praying for Shanna to get the business she needed. He could see a good ending to the story except for Ray. That was what bothered him. He knew she hadn't wanted him to witness anything about her personal life, but it had happened. He'd become involved whether he wanted to be or not. If anything happened to Shanna, now that he'd seen Ray in action, Brendan wouldn't be able to live with himself. He didn't think it was wrong to want her to be happy, just like she was now, playfully kissing her daffy dog. The only thing he would change in this picture was that instead of the dog kissing her, it would be himself, and he would be kissing her properly.

The realization of what he wanted to do made his breath catch. His life's plans didn't include a ready-made home and family. He wanted to start his own "happily-ever-after" without having to carry someone else's baggage.

He cleared his throat, causing her to hold the dog still and look up at him.

"Jeff told me you need to work with Boffo every day until the next lesson, because we can't have him just listening to me. He said Boffo's already made good progress, just in the first two-hour class."

Jeff had also said that Brendan, too, had to be diligent with the daily lesson plan, since he was the one taking Boffo to the dog school. Brendan didn't mind that, though. He definitely wanted to change a few of Boffo's habits, most important, his digging. Otherwise, the beauty of what he was doing would be spoiled and end up no different than before he started.

For now, except for the seams, the newly sodded lawn was rock solid against digging marauders. In a couple of months, though, when the roots took hold of the ground below and many waterings had loosened the original layer of soil, Boffo would be able to dislodge it enough to dig holes.

Brendan pulled the class instruction sheet from his back

pocket. "Let's go over this while it's fresh in my mind. The first things we're supposed to work on are *sit*, *down*, and *heel*." He showed her how to prompt the dog to do everything he'd been shown in class, then released Boffo from the leash. "Jeff said the biggest motivation for the dog is praise. At first, give him treats; but later just a pat and a kind word will be all we need. Now I have to get to work. The materials for the playscape will be here in an hour, and I've got to get ready."

For once it was Brendan, not Boffo, who did the digging. Using his power auger, after taking the measurements twice, he dug the holes he was going to need for the support posts. Next, he hauled the bags of cement and mixing tubs to where they would be needed. With perfect timing, the delivery truck arrived in front of the house when he was ready.

Moving the materials for the playscape was considerably less work than lugging 160 rolls of sod. By the time Shanna returned after picking up Matthew from kindergarten, Brendan had the frame in place. The children, and Boffo, too, sat still, fascinated, as he put the set together piece by piece. Their eyes lit up when the slide was in place. He warned them not to touch the pieces of the fort section that he'd laid out in the order he needed for assembly. Even though it nearly killed them, they obeyed.

For once, Boffo didn't take off with any tools, allowing Brendan to finish the playscape in record time. He poured the cement around the posts, then helped Matthew and Ashley write their names. Brendan finished the job by writing the day's date.

"That's it," he said as he swiped his hands down the

sides of his jeans. "All I have left to do is put the swing up when the cement is set, paint it, and we're done. So today, you can look at your new playscape, but don't climb on it quite yet."

While the kids squealed and ran around the playscape, snaking underneath the fort section and circling the support posts, Brendan looked at the faded fence.

His feelings of self-satisfaction faded.

When he'd first started this job, he'd mentally noted its poor condition. Shanna had asked him to repair a few sections that were at the point of falling down, but no more. Harry had been very clear not to mention any extra work that he thought should be done, because she simply couldn't afford it. Fixing up the yard and making it presentable for her business clients was all he was to do. But now it wasn't enough. After the new playscape was painted, the fence would look even worse by comparison.

He walked across the freshly laid lawn and poked at a section of the old fence. Many of the boards at the back were starting to rot because they'd only been painted on one side, which was the worst thing anyone could do. By next year, especially if they had another windstorm, a section or two would come down.

Just painting the fence wouldn't be good enough. She needed a new one.

He turned to watch Shanna through the window, alternately hunched over her computer, then digging through the second box of his disorganized receipts and paperwork.

He knew that when he was done working in her yard, it would be at least another month before she was finished with his bookkeeping and tax returns. Of course, the deal for Shanna was the cost of her time, while he'd had to pay actual money for the materials. Still, this was more than a job or just a barter for services rendered. He wanted everything to be perfect for her, and the only thing in his power to change was her yard—it was his contribution to brighten her future.

Until the fence was as good as the rest, the project was incomplete, whether she agreed or not. But at the same time, he had other projects contracted—projects that paid the wage he needed to pay his rent, car payment, and groceries. Projects that he'd promised to have completed by specific dates.

He hated to, but he had no choice. He'd already crossed the line from business-only to personal. Now it was going to get even more personal.

Brendan pulled out his cell phone and typed out a text message. He cringed as he hit SEND, telling himself he was only doing this because he had obligations to meet and promises to keep.

It was done.

◈

For the first time in months, Shanna was alone.

She'd taken both the children to visit friends for a few hours. Brendan was away on his lunch break.

The yard was deserted except for Boffo, who was lying in the cool, new grass, sleeping in the shade of the new playscape. Boffo let out a quiet "woof" in his sleep, his tail thumped, and he again quieted in his doggy dreamland. She wondered if he was dreaming of going to dog school with Brendan.

Brendan.

The dog liked him and the kids loved him.

Shanna didn't know quite how to feel about him, except that he made her nervous.

Brendan was a laborer. Everything he did required physical force and strength. She'd never seen such muscles except on bodybuilders on television infomercials, which probably weren't even real. But Brendan's strength and power were very real. The speed at which Ray had retreated when Brendan confronted him was proof of that—and her best incentive never to be on the wrong side of Brendan's fury. It was a lesson she'd taken too long to learn with Roger, and it was a mistake she'd never repeat.

Shanna had tried to act like the good wife she should have been, but she didn't know how. Most of her friends were also newlyweds, and they were too starry-eyed from being recently married to give her any practical advice. The only example of a long-term marriage she had to follow was that of her parents, but Shanna didn't want her marriage to be like that. Her mother couldn't do anything to make her father happy. Shanna had countless memories of her parents fighting, with her mother always coming out the loser. As a child, she had rationalized what she'd seen, likening such scenarios to a parent punishing a bad child. As an adult, she now knew how wrong that was. She'd never seen her father hit her mother, but that didn't mean it didn't happen. Her mother spent a lot of time crying. She seemed to live her life for the sole purpose of not making her husband angry.

Shanna didn't want her marriage to be the same, so she made sure she'd married a man who wasn't a perfectionist like her father—she didn't want to be partnered with someone who would think nothing she did was good enough. Instead, Roger became bored with her, then frustrated. Then he began pushing her around, and the cycle continued. In the end, she'd married a man not much different than her father. Roger's death hadn't relieved her of being victimized. Roger's whole family was the same, including his parents, and his brother was the same way to his wife that Roger had been to her. Bigger, stronger, smarter, and everyone had to know it.

She'd easily fallen in love with Roger. He oozed power and masculinity. He made her feel safe, because no one would dare confront him. But then she'd learned the hard way that she couldn't confront Roger, either. To him, confrontation meant disagreeing with him. She would never again be so blind or so gullible. She would never let herself fall into that trap again. When she began dating again, she would seek out a man who was quiet, understated, and gentle, whose biggest strength was his faith, not his might.

The chime on her wristwatch sounded, signaling it was 1:00, the official end of Brendan's lunch break. Right on time, his pickup pulled up to the front of the house.

The sound roused Boffo from his sleep. The dog bounded to the gate, then sat waiting. His only movement was his tail swooshing behind him.

Shanna could barely believe Boffo's good behavior. Brendan was doing wonders with the dog in a remarkably short amount of time.

He was also doing wonders with her children. She'd bartered good behavior from them, and even a few household chores, for the privilege of spending time with Brendan in the yard. Even better, by taking the children into the yard while he worked, Brendan was helping her get more done by keeping them busy. He was teaching Boffo to be not only a good pet, but a potential watchdog, as well. And if it wasn't her imagination, the playscape was much larger than what she thought he'd originally described. A truckload of wood had arrived this morning, which meant Brendan wasn't just replacing the one section that was ready to fall down; she was getting a whole new fence.

She didn't know how she could ever pay him back. The only thing she could do was to do more work for him, which meant spending more time with him. And that was exactly what she didn't want. She'd fallen for his type before; only this time she knew the risks and her own mistakes, and especially her weaknesses.

This time, Shanna was going to put a stop to it while she could. Already she regretted that he'd seen her vulnerability with Ray. She didn't want to seem ungrateful for everything extra that Brendan was doing, but it was time to stop him from becoming any more involved with her personal life. She would thank him for his help with the dog, but she would take Boffo to dog school herself and pay for babysitting. She would find something else for her children to do instead of letting them pretend to help him work. The second he came into the yard, she would also tell him that while she appreciated his offer, she really didn't need a new fence and that their business together was nearly complete.

The gate opened and Brendan stepped inside, but before she could speak, a second person walked in behind him. A woman was with him. Both Brendan and the woman stopped. He rested one hand on the woman's shoulder. "Shanna, I'd like you to meet my mother."

five

Shanna's heart stopped beating.

She remembered when Roger had introduced her to his mother. Looking back, that was her signal that Roger intended to make the relationship serious.

She didn't want a serious relationship. She didn't want any relationship. Especially not with King Kong.

"Hi," she said, unable to keep her voice from coming out like a strangled squeak.

"Shanna?" Brendan asked, stepping forward. "Are you okay? Is something wrong?"

Shanna shook her head, then nodded as she gulped in a deep breath of air, trying to force her heart to start beating again. "I'm fine," she choked out. "I'm sorry. I was just thinking of. . .something." She turned to his mother. "I'm pleased to meet you."

His mother smiled and extended one hand. "My name is Kathy. Are you sure you're okay?"

"Yes. I'm so sorry."

Absently, Brendan lifted his hand and stroked his beard. "I have another project to start today. My mother often does painting for me when I need help. If you don't mind, I'm going to leave her here and pick her up on my way back."

"N—no. . .I don't mind."

"Great. I just have to get the paint out of my truck."

The second Brendan disappeared, Kathy started talking. "I've heard a lot about your new playscape. As usual, it looks better than Brendan described it. He's too modest with the things he does. I see he's done a lovely job of your yard, too."

Even though she'd already looked at it a million times, Shanna took in the transformation, still barely able to believe it was real. The ground was now perfectly even, and the grass was green and lush. A row of small shrubs—azaleas, rhododendrons, some rosebushes, and a few ferns lined the back fence, completing the picture. Brendan told her he'd selected these particular plants so she could have a beautiful array of flowers from early spring until late fall.

The two rock gardens splashed more color into her yard. These were planted with hardy dark green shrubs and a rainbow of pansies. They were both artistic and beautiful. The corner flower bed was constructed with plastic covering the ground and plants poking out from cut holes, the plastic covered by mulch. Brendan had explained that he'd done it like this so she wouldn't have weeds to pull from around the plants.

In both corners he'd planted a couple of bushes. She couldn't remember the technical name he'd given her, but the common name was butterfly bush. Over the years they would become big and lush, and for most of the summer and into the fall they would be loaded with cascading purple blossoms. This was one of Brendan's favorite perennials because it was hardy and fragrant. As the name implied, it would attract butterflies. Around both trees he'd planted a mixture of bright blossoms—carnations, marigolds, petunias, and a number of others she couldn't remember the names of. He'd said this was the only place he'd planted annuals because he'd also planted a variety of bulbs for the earliest of the spring flowers—daffodils in all their color variations, tulips, and crocuses. She just wouldn't be able to see those until next year. And as a special touch, under the eaves, he'd hung a few pots of brilliant pink and white fuchsias that were supposed to attract hummingbirds.

"Uh. . .yes. . .he's done a great job."

Brendan returned with two cans of paint, far too much to cover just the playscape—probably enough to start work on the fence when it was completed.

He checked his wristwatch. "I'll see you at 5:00."

He was gone before she could respond.

Kathy waved one hand in the air. "Don't mind me. Go back to work. Don't be afraid to let the children into the yard. I'll keep them off the wet paint. I know I'll enjoy their company while I do this. I'm not even going to call it work. I love painting even more than I love knitting. I can tell you that it's much more difficult to find a painting job than it is to go to the store and buy a couple of skeins of wool."

Shanna glanced toward the empty playscape. "Actually, my children aren't home. As you can see, it's just me and my dog."

Kathy turned her head to watch Boffo, who was sitting at the gate Brendan had just left through, waiting for him to come back.

One corner of Kathy's mouth tipped up. "So that's the. . . uh"—Kathy paused and cleared her throat—"*large* dog he's been taking to Jeff's obedience class."

Shanna's cheeks warmed, thinking that Brendan had

probably used other words to describe Boffo. "That would be him."

Kathy rubbed her hands together. "This is getting better. And it's making more and more sense."

"I don't understand."

"He talks differently about you than his other landscaping clients." Kathy giggled. "He said that you and I would get along like peanut butter and jam."

"I beg your pardon?"

"I'm just repeating what he said."

Memories of what Roger had said about his mother poked into Shanna's mind. Roger had also told Shanna that his mother would like her, although not in that way. At the time, Shanna had been flattered. It had been less flattering when Roger's mother started asking too-personal questions, then began snooping around her house to see what kind of wife Shanna would be to her precious son. In hindsight, Shanna now knew that Roger's mother was looking for someone who would be a perfect housekeeper, because Roger was such a slob. Roger had laughed it off, and not long after that, they were married.

However, this time Shanna wasn't meeting the mother of a man she wanted to marry. This was the mother of someone with whom she had made a business agreement—and Shanna wanted it to stay that way. Yet, despite her hesitations, her impression was that Brendan didn't have any hidden agenda with leaving his mother to paint the playscape. Kathy was simply there to work. There was even the possibility that since his mother said she enjoyed painting, Brendan was doing his mother a favor by providing something she liked to do.

The smart thing would be to back off and not answer any personal questions—and only let Brendan's mother into the house when she had to use the bathroom.

Kathy picked up a can of paint and a brush. "So, tell me, Shanna, do you knit?"

Shanna's gaze met Kathy's and held. Her impression of Kathy was that, unlike Roger's mother, Kathy was sincere, and her question wasn't personal; it was simply to start a light conversation. In a way, Kathy reminded Shanna of an older version of her pastor's wife. "I knit a little," Shanna muttered, not wanting to be rude. "I'm not very good."

Kathy pried the lid off the paint can. "I knit a lot. If you want, I can help you. I have boxes of adorable patterns in my collection that kids fall in love with."

"Really?" Shanna asked before she could stop herself. When Kathy looked up and smiled, something inside of Shanna started to melt. Brendan's mother wasn't grilling Shanna about how she spent her time. She was just offering to help.

"Yes," Kathy replied. "I have patterns from beginner up to advanced." She smiled again, the crinkles at the corners of her eyes reminding Shanna of one of the elderly ladies at church whose biggest joy in life was spending time with younger women, either nurturing them or just having fun.

Kathy looked at her, waiting, until Shanna felt awkward about not responding. "I'm definitely a beginner," she mumbled. "I tried and tried, but it wouldn't work, so I gave up."

"You probably gave up too soon. All you need is someone to show you how. We have a ladies' group at my church that gets together for coffee once a month, and many of the ladies bring their knitting. I've shown a number of them how to do the pictures, and I could show you, too. Don't be shy. I don't bite."

Guilt surged through Shanna's heart. She had been completely unfair, as well as judgmental. Brendan's mother wasn't there to spy on her; she just wanted to be friendly.

Shanna gathered her courage. "Matthew has a friend who gets new sweaters with all his favorite cartoon characters on them. He was so disappointed when I couldn't do it."

"Most of the ones for young children aren't that difficult. The secret is using a ruler."

"A ruler?"

"I'll show you. Brendan will be here to pick me up later, but I can always come back in the evening myself. Or another day."

Shanna nibbled on her bottom lip. Matthew would be deliriously happy to get a sweater with a picture on it, handmade by his mother. Ashley didn't have a favorite cartoon character, but she loved sheep or anything with a sheep on it. A friend had given Shanna a pattern to knit a toy sheep, but she hadn't been able to figure it out. If Kathy could knit pictures into a sweater, surely she could help Shanna knit a sheep.

Dear Lord, please tell me I'm not being foolish to trust this woman. Tell me that I'm doing the right thing.

She had to rely on God, that He was opening a new door that led to a place where she would be safe.

"As long as it's not too much trouble, that would be nice. Thank you."

Kathy smiled warmly. "I think it will be fun. Now you

get back to work in your office, and I'll get busy. I'll see you later."

Shanna returned to her desk, but instead of checking her client's expense figures, she watched Kathy painting. On first impression, she liked Brendan's mother. Thinking about Kathy's offer, Shanna knew she really did need a friend. While the women at church were nice, and she certainly enjoyed herself every few months when she participated in a function with them, she wasn't close to anyone there. Mostly, it was her own fault. When she was married to Roger, he hadn't wanted to go to church. He'd go only on Christmas and Mother's Day. Other than that, she took the children on her own. All the ladies there were married, so she felt awkward at family functions without Roger. And while she had some fellowship, she didn't have anyone she could really talk to or any true friendship. The issues she had to deal with weren't something she could share, so she kept mostly to herself.

But this was different. Like Shanna, Kathy was alone. Matthew had told her that Brendan didn't have a daddy anymore, either. Shanna could only assume that Kathy had chosen to remain single. At some point, Shanna would marry again, but for now she didn't want a boyfriend. But she did need a friend. Perhaps Kathy did, too.

Shanna watched Brendan's mother dipping the paintbrush into the can. She wondered if Kathy was lonely now that her son was grown up and not living in her home anymore.

Shanna couldn't imagine living alone. Being a self-employed, single mother was busy—very busy. Today was a rare day; both children were gone and everything was quiet. Boffo was even behaving himself, sitting quietly watching Kathy paint while Kathy talked to him. He even seemed to be listening and responding to what she said.

But her work wasn't going to get done if she spent the day staring out the window. As she should have done earlier, Shanna took advantage of the silence and got busy.

Halfway through the afternoon, Shanna poured two glasses of iced tea and joined Kathy.

As she walked, she looked up to the top of the fort section of the playscape, noticing for the first time that Brendan had put shingles on the roof—the same shingles that were on her house.

The paint Kathy had applied was exactly the same color as the trim around the windows.

The man didn't miss anything.

She handed Kathy the glass. "I thought we could both use a break."

"Thanks. This will really hit the spot."

Shanna made sure the ground was dry enough; then she lowered herself to sit in the soft, new grass. "Do you do a lot of this kind of thing?"

Kathy shook her head. "Not as much as I'd like. Brendan doesn't get a lot of jobs like your playscape. Usually, if he builds anything, it's just fences made with pretreated wood, so there's no paint needed. He's seeing a new trend with chain-link fences, so now there's even less for me to paint. I like to help him. I'm also very efficient with a seeder."

"I guess you don't have another job? After all, you're here in the afternoon."

"I have a full-time job, but it's retail, so the hours and days are flexible. I'm only here today because this week

I have to work Saturday. Fortunately for me, it's a small, privately owned store, so I don't have to work on Sundays. After church I like to spend the day with my friends, especially in the summer. I try to keep myself busy. I'm sure you know what it's like. Brendan tells me that you're a widow, too."

"Uh, yes, I am."

Kathy smiled, but her eyes lost focus. "You've got your children to keep you busy. I only had one child, and he's all grown up now. He still keeps me busy, but in different ways. He's a wonderful boy."

The image of Brendan towering above her formed a very clear picture in Shanna's mind. Brendan Gafferty was far from a "boy."

Kathy drank some of the iced tea, then lowered the glass, setting it in the grass so it wouldn't spill while she painted. "I should let you get back to work. Brendan says you're very busy now that you've taken him on as a client of sorts."

Shanna rose, brushing a few loose blades of grass off her clothes as she stood. "Yes, he's right about that. We can talk more tonight when you come back." As the words left her mouth, she knew they were true. She missed being involved in an adult conversation with someone who had no expectations of her and wanted nothing in return.

Kathy walked to her paint can and dipped in the brush. "Brendan should be back in another hour. I only have a little left to do, so I wanted to get this finished. I'll come back later, after supper."

Shanna smiled. "That sounds like fun." As the words left her mouth, her smile widened. It really did sound like fun, and she could hardly wait for Kathy to come back.

Brendan told himself not to worry when his mother didn't answer her house phone. But then, when her cell phone went to voice mail, he told himself not to panic. He wasn't calling about anything important. But it was important that she wasn't home. Tonight was Thursday night. His mother was always home on Thursday night to watch her favorite television program. And even if she wasn't home, she always answered her cell phone. Before he assumed she was lying on the floor unable to get up, he tried one last thing before he drove to her house to check on her.

Brendan corrected four errors while typing the message, but he finally entered the words and text-messaged his mother on his cell phone.

Where are you?

He waited one long minute for a response, but instead of simply ringing to be answered, the phone signaled the tone for a text message.

I'm at Shanna's house. We're busy. Can't talk. I'll see you tomorrow.

Brendan stared at the message in disbelief. Not only had she not phoned back, but her text message was blunt and she didn't want to talk to him. Also, if he hadn't been mistaken, his mother had been at Shanna's house every day that week. He stared at the message until it timed out and the screen went blank.

Brendan had wanted his mother to make new friends, but in hindsight, he should have seen this coming. His mother had plenty of friends at church, but there almost every friend she had was half of a couple. His mother often felt the odd person out, regardless of how friendly everyone was and how well they treated her. The bottom line was that she was the only person at most of the occasions who was single. She refused to attend the singles group because everyone there was too young for her; namely, they were his age, not his mother's age. But lately she'd begun to turn down invitations to functions she normally attended. After all these years of being single, it was starting to wear on her. And it was starting to worry Brendan.

Brendan wanted very much for his mother to find a good friend who was another single woman. He'd felt that his mother and Shanna would get along well, but he hadn't envisioned them connecting like this.

Still, Shanna and his mother had a lot in common. Not that he talked a lot to Shanna, but her kids talked a lot about her while they "helped" him in the backyard. Besides the obvious similarities, as listed by her children, neither Shanna nor his mother had a man in her life, nor were they making any effort to find one. Shanna had even declined his invitation to attend his church's singles group with him. He'd almost taken the fast rejection personally, but he reminded himself of what Matthew had told him about other men she'd also turned down.

Brendan snapped his phone shut, but he'd no sooner fastened it back on his belt when it sang the familiar ring tone, this time signaling that it wasn't a text message, but a real caller.

The display showed his mother's cell number.

"Brendan? I need you to come to Shanna's right away."

The urgency in her voice made his heart skip a beat. His mother was one person who could always be relied upon in the case of an emergency. He'd suffered terrible allergies as a child, and his mother's quick action had saved him from death more than once. His first thought was that something had happened to one of Shanna's children. In that case, she should be calling an ambulance, not him. "What's wrong? Should I bring something? What do you need?"

"I need *you*. Come now. Hurry. But don't speed. I don't want you getting a ticket, or worse."

He abandoned his half-eaten supper on the table and ran out the door. A ticket would be the least of his worries; but he wouldn't be any good to anyone, especially in an emergency, if he was late or had an accident and injured himself or someone else.

The traffic lights were on his side. Brendan arrived at Shanna's home in good time. He ran to the door, opened it without knocking, and dashed in.

The second his foot touched the floor, Boffo came bounding down the stairs. Brendan pushed down on Boffo's shoulders to make the dog remember to sit and not jump on people, and Brendan raised his head. "Mom? Shanna? Where are you?" he called up the stairs.

His mother and Shanna hustled down the stairs, both wearing jackets. The children were nowhere to be seen. In the background, he heard the television, but it wasn't *CSI*; it was a cartoon.

"Susan called. I forgot all about the ladies' Snack 'n Yak night. We need you to watch the children."

Shanna smiled weakly. "They both go to bed at 7:30, 8:00 at the latest, or Matthew will be cranky in the morning."

Brendan froze where he stood. "You called me here in a big rush so you could go have coffee with a bunch of women?"

"It's more than that. This is part of our big fund-raising project. It's the dessert auction. We've raised a lot of money for that orphanage the church is sponsoring, but we still need more. Fortunately, Shanna had just made a batch of cupcakes for the children, so we're taking most of those tonight. I hope we have enough larger cakes for the auction, but there's nothing I can do about that now. Susan just called and said a couple of the people who volunteered to help got sick. Shanna said she could help, so we need you to watch Matthew and Ashley. You don't mind, do you?"

"Well. . . I. . ."

"I hear that Rosie is making her famous triple chocolate delight cake. If you give me some money, I'll see if I can bid on it for you."

Brendan knew he'd lost the battle. There was no point in trying to fight. He reached into his back pocket for his wallet and gave his mother twice as much as he thought any self-respecting cake should go for.

After she took his money, his mother reached up to rest her hands on his shoulders. She rose on her tiptoes, pulling him down slightly as she stretched herself out to as much height as she could manage, then gave him a quick peck on the cheek. "You're a dear. We'll see you later. Bye."

Before he could respond, both women were gone and the door closed behind them.

"I don't believe this," he muttered to the wall.

His mother's car started, and within seconds, they were gone.

Brendan turned his head and listened to what was going on upstairs before he actually went up.

He'd never been inside Shanna's house before, except for the brief time it took to get rid of her brother-in-law. Otherwise, he'd only been in the office, through the entrance from the backyard.

He looked up the stairs. Shanna's home was like many others in suburban Seattle—a two-story house with a ground-level entry and the main living area on the upper floor. He was a little familiar with the ground level. It was smaller because it was cut out for the garage and consisted of her office, another small room, a small bathroom, and the main entrance foyer where the stairs accessed the living area.

Before walking up, he peeked to his left, around the corner to see what she had done with the other room he'd never seen.

It appeared to be a makeshift family room with inexpensive carpeting laid on top of the cement floor. A worn, color-dated sofa and an old television lined the walls, and the floor was strewn with the children's and Boffo's toys. On the other side of the room there was a small work space with the washer, dryer, and a laundry sink, all of which butted up to the bathroom wall, for the functionality of keeping the plumbing centrally located. Next to this was another door opening, which led to Shanna's office at the rear of the house. The setup wasn't pretty, but it was functional, and mostly, it worked.

He walked up the stairs, where he found Matthew sitting on the living room floor surrounded by plastic bricks, half his attention on the television and half on what appeared to be the beginnings of a boat. Ashley was curled up in one corner of the couch, hugging a stuffed bear, her gaze glued completely to the television.

"Hi, kids," he said, making his best attempt to sound cheerful.

They both nodded, but neither spoke or broke their attention away from their show.

Beside him, Boffo wagged his tail and pressed his cold, wet nose into Brendan's hand.

One big, happy family. It almost made him want to call out, "Honey, I'm home," but there was no "honey," and it wasn't his home. He didn't belong here, but he couldn't leave. He could only stare at the children. Outside, in the backyard, he could keep them busy. Here, in their home, he didn't know what to do. So he sat on the couch and watched the cartoon with them.

He wasn't quite sure how or when it happened, but an hour later, Ashley had wiggled over and was lying with her head in his lap, hugging her bear, fast asleep. Matthew was on his other side, leaning against him, holding a now fully made boat limply in one hand, also sleeping. Boffo lay in front of him, on top of his feet. Not only was Boffo sleeping, but he was also snoring. Brendan wondered when he'd become so boring.

Instead of spending the evening being used as an oversized pillow, he steadied Matthew, wiggled his feet out from underneath Boffo, and shuffled sideways on the couch so he could slip away from Ashley without waking her. Assured that she was still sleeping and that she wouldn't fall off the couch, he carried Matthew into the hallway. The first door on the left was a bedroom done in shades of pinks and purples, so he kept going. The next door on the right was definitely an adult bedroom, although he did see some clothes on the floor and the bed wasn't made.

The next door was the bathroom, and after that, a bedroom painted with bright primary colors, spotted with posters of racing cars and monster trucks. Scattered on the floor was a variety of cars, trucks, and miscellaneous action figures. A well-used stuffed bear lay haphazardly on the bed.

Brendan pushed the covers down, then very gently laid Matthew on the bed.

He stood straight and looked down. He didn't want to wake the child, but he didn't think he should leave Matthew fully dressed on his bed. But then, Matthew wasn't his child, and he didn't want to do anything that might frighten the boy, which probably included tugging off his clothes.

Brendan arranged the blankets over Matthew loosely, thinking that if Matthew woke up in the middle of the night, he could change into his pajamas by himself.

He hurried back to the living room, but neither Ashley nor Boffo had moved. He did the same with Ashley as he had done with Matthew, thinking it was probably even more important to leave Ashley to dress herself.

When he returned to the living room, Boffo hadn't moved, although one eye was half open.

"Well, dog," he muttered. "Looks like it's just you and me. We seem to be seeing a lot of each other, don't we?"

Boffo's tail thumped once on the floor; otherwise, he still didn't move.

"I guess that's once for yes, twice for no."

Brendan sat on the couch, then rose to walk around the

small living room, searching for the remote.

"You didn't bury that somewhere, too, did you?" Brendan muttered as he lifted the newspapers on the coffee table, then the couch cushions. He finally found it on the carpet, half under the couch.

He sat, aimed, and began flipping channels.

"Has Shanna been going over your lessons? I hope you've been listening to her." He already knew the answer. He'd seen an improvement in Boffo's behavior, and so had his friend who ran the dog school. So he knew Boffo's reply would have been a resounding yes.

He waited for Boffo to thump his tail once, but it didn't happen. "So how have things been all week?"

The dog sighed, keeping his chin resting on his paws.

"That good, huh? Same here."

Boffo shifted. Brendan wondered if perhaps one of the children had become restless. He turned his head and looked down the hall, but all was silent. When he turned back to Boffo, he saw that the dog had rolled onto his side.

"I guess that means no worries. That's good, because I've never been a babysitter before. When I was a teen, I made extra money by cutting lawns, which is probably how I got my start into what I'm doing now."

Boffo sighed again, and his eyes closed.

Brendan wondered what had happened, that he was now talking to a dog. It wasn't even his dog.

"I want a glass of water," a sleepy little voice called from down the hall.

Immediately Brendan rose, intending to get Ashley her glass of water before she woke up completely and wouldn't be able to get back to sleep. But in his haste, he forgot about Boffo sprawled out on the floor. One foot caught under one of Boffo's legs, nearly sending Brendan headfirst into the television. He recovered his balance, grumbled to himself, and continued into Ashley's bedroom.

He stood in the doorway. "I'll make you a deal. If you put your pajamas on and get back into bed real nice, I'll get you a glass of water real fast."

Ashley yawned. "Okay."

Once in the kitchen, Brendan stared at the cupboards. He didn't know where the glasses were, but he didn't want to snoop. Even though he was doing Shanna a favor, he didn't want to do anything that might be considered invasive.

He took a guess as to where the glasses were and guessed correctly. As he pulled a glass out, he smiled, noting how the contents were organized. The glasses were on the bottom shelf, mugs on the middle shelf, and on the top were obscure things that looked like they hadn't been touched for ages. He had no trouble reaching anything on the top shelf, but he had a feeling Shanna did, which was why the top shelf appeared to be used only for storage.

He wondered what else she considered inaccessible.

To give Ashley more time to change, he indulged his curiosity. He bent his knees in a semi-squat until he guessed that he was now at Shanna's height, and surveyed the small room.

Everything looked and felt different—as if he were standing in a hole.

Keeping his knees bent, he shuffled around the kitchen, gaining a new perspective.

"What are you doing? Are you okay?"

Brendan straightened as fast as if he'd jumped, then spun around to see Matthew in the entrance to the hall, staring at him as if he'd lost his marbles.

Feeling his ears grow hot, Brendan cleared his throat. "I thought I'd see what things looked like from your mother's height."

"Huh?"

Brendan looked down at Matthew. He didn't know enough about children in general to be able to judge if Matthew was short or tall for his age. Shanna wasn't really short, but she wasn't tall, either. Judging from the heights of the women at church, he figured she was just a little shorter than average, but not much. Brendan, on the other hand, had been tall all his life, from elementary school to high school, always the tallest in every class. He'd always sat in the back row and had always been first pick for sports teams.

Brendan lowered himself so that one knee rested on the floor. He still hovered above Matthew, but there was nothing he could do. "When you grow up, you're going to have to help your mom reach stuff. It's a good thing to be able to help. Just remember how special your mom is and how good it is that God gave you such a special mom."

Matthew's eyes widened. "Tyler in my class doesn't have a mom. Or a dad, either. He lives with his grandma."

Brendan didn't know, and he didn't want to ask the reasons for that, because there were many possibilities. "How would you like to pray for Tyler tonight?"

Matthew yawned and nodded. Brendan patted his shoulder, then stood.

"As soon as I get that glass of water for your sister, we can say your prayers. Go to your room and put your pajamas on while I give this to Ashley, and I'll be right there."

Matthew wasted no time returning to his room. By the time Brendan walked into Ashley's room, he could tell she was changed, because her clothes were scattered on the floor, including a sock on each side of the dresser, and she was sitting in the middle of the bed waiting for him. She noisily gulped down the water, then flopped down onto her back.

Brendan hoped the burst of energy wasn't going to hinder Ashley from going back to sleep. He leaned forward to brush a lock of hair out of her eyes. "Would you like to say your prayers? When I was your age, my mom always prayed with me before bed."

Ashley squeezed her eyes shut and folded her hands beneath her chin. "Dear God, thank You for my mommy and my brother and for Boffo and for all my toys, especially my bear, and for Mr. Brendan who is making our yard look really good. And thank You for our new slide and fort in the backyard, which is almost finished, amen."

"Amen," Brendan said in agreement and stood.

"Isn't you gonna kiss me good night?"

"Uh. . .I guess so."

He bent down and pressed a gentle kiss onto Ashley's forehead. Just as he was about to straighten, she flung her arms around him as best she could reach, and squeezed with all her childlike strength, which wasn't much, but it came from the depths of her little heart. "Good night, Mr. Brendan. I like you really lots. Is you gonna come back tomorrow?"

"Probably. I have another job to do someplace else, but it won't take me long. Then I'll be back to work on the fence for your mother. So yes. I'll be back tomorrow."

"Good. I misses you."

He smiled. "I've missed you, too." Strangely, he found he wasn't saying the words as a reassuring platitude—he really meant them. "Now, if you'll let me go, I'm going to go pray with your brother."

She released him and rolled over onto her side. "Good night, Mr. Brendan," she muttered, and settled in for the night.

"Good night, Ashley."

On his way out, he pulled the door until it was only open a crack and made his way to Matthew's room.

The second he knelt beside Matthew's bed, Matthew closed his eyes and folded his hands beneath his chin, just as Ashley had, which made Brendan smile.

"Dear God, thank You for my mommy and thank You for Tyler's grandma who takes care of him. Also thank You for Missus Kathy. . ." Matthew's voice trailed off. His eyes sprang open, and he looked at Brendan. "Missus Kathy is your mommy, not your grandma, right?"

Brendan bit his tongue, wondering what his mother would think of Matthew's innocent question. "Yes, Missus Kathy is my mommy."

"Okay." Matthew resumed his position and reclosed his eyes. "And thank You for Mr. Brendan's mommy, Missus Kathy. She's a nice lady, and she's having fun painting our new fort. Thank You for the sweater she's helping Mommy knit that they don't think I know about, and thank You for the cookies Missus Kathy brought today. They were really yummy, amen."

"My mother brought cookies?"

Matthew nodded. "Yes. She said they were your favorite cookies when you was my age."

Brendan stared at the boy. "She brought you my favorite chocolate chip cookies? The ones with peanut butter in them?" When he was a child, he'd often made those cookies with his mother. After he moved out, she still made them for him; only she usually ended up eating too many before his next visit, then blamed Brendan that she'd gained five pounds. "Are there any left?"

"No. My mommy ate the last one. Missus Kathy said that when your daddy died, you were very sad, and cookies made you feel better."

He didn't know if it was exactly the cookies or the time spent with his mother making them. "Yes, I was sad for a long time." He didn't know what to say to Matthew, but he had been devastated when his father died. "You must miss your dad a lot" was the best he could come up with.

"I guess. He didn't like to play with us, and lots of times he made Mommy cry. I didn't like it when he made Mommy cry."

Brendan's stomach clenched. "Do you know why he made her cry?"

"He yelled at us a lot. He yelled at Mommy, too, and called her bad names. That made her cry lots of times."

Matthew's answer wasn't specific, but it did give Brendan a little insight. It also made him wonder if such behavior ran in the family, after witnessing Matthew's uncle Ray in action.

"I think it's past the time that your mom said you should be in bed."

"I'm in bed."

"But you're not sleeping. Close your eyes."

Brendan gave Matthew a quick hug and returned to the living room.

Boffo was still lying on the carpet in front of the couch in the identical position he had been in when Brendan had left him nearly half an hour ago.

"Why can't you be more like this during the day?" he muttered as he lowered the volume on the television.

Brendan flopped down on the couch and watched reruns until Boffo sprang to his feet and ran to the window. The sudden movement caused Brendan to wonder what was wrong, so he joined the dog at the window.

Nothing seemed amiss. The only movement was that his mother's car had returned and both doors opened.

He stood at the top of the stairs. When the door opened, Shanna and his mother walked in, both carrying cake boxes.

"How come I didn't get any cookies?" he called down the stairs. The amount of money he'd given his mother for the cake flashed through his mind, reminding him that he now had to go to the ATM on the way home. "I hope one of those boxes is for me."

His mother had the nerve to laugh. "I hope you don't mind, but I gave half the cake to Shanna and then took a bit for myself." She set the box on the bottom step. "But don't worry. There's a nice piece left for you. I'm going home now. Will you be back here tomorrow so you can work on Shanna's fence?"

"Yes."

"Then good night. Here's your cake, but you have to make your own cookies. I gave you the recipe years ago."

Before he could think of an appropriate response, she was gone, leaving him alone with Shanna. She toed off her shoes and walked up the stairs, carrying the box containing half of what was supposed to be *his* cake.

"Were the kids okay? I can't remember the last time I left them. They've never had anyone else put them to bed. I hope there wasn't a lot of crying."

Crying? The thought hadn't occurred to him. It made him glad he hadn't known that before she left.

She walked past him, then padded down the hall, still holding the box. She peeked into the bedrooms as if she needed confirmation that they really were sleeping soundly.

"There were no problems. Maybe they were thinking it was like when their dad put them to bed."

"Their father never put them to bed," she said, her voice suddenly sharp. "Most of the time he wasn't home when it was their bedtime."

"Oh. Did he work late shifts?"

"No. He just chose not to come home."

It sounded like a line he wasn't meant to cross, so Brendan changed the subject. "I think it's time for me to leave. I'll be back to work on your fence tomorrow, so I'll probably see you sometime after lunch. I'll just pick up the world's most expensive piece of cake and see myself out."

six

Shanna could tell the exact second Brendan arrived.

First, Boffo began to run in circles behind her, whining. Next, he ran outside through the special doggy door that Brendan had made in the screen. His behavior alerted the children, and recognizing the signs, they both dropped whatever they were doing and ran to the gate to wait for their hero.

Shanna set down her pencil, but she didn't run to greet him.

Part of her was happy that her children finally had a good male role model, at least when Brendan was at his best, working by daylight in their backyard. So far they hadn't seen him when he was tired after a long day and his patience was tested. Nor had she, and she wanted to keep it that way. She didn't ever want to be on the wrong side of Brendan's anger, especially after experiencing what it was like to be on the wrong side of Roger's anger. After a few trips to the hospital, Shanna had promised herself, and God, that she would never permit herself or her children to be in that predicament again.

The night that Kathy had called Brendan to come watch the children while they rushed off to the forgotten charity fund-raiser, she'd thanked God from the bottom of her heart that it hadn't been a bad day for him. He'd been so sweet and a willing helper, and she didn't want to do anything to change that. When she and Brendan went their separate ways, she wanted Ashley and Matthew to have good memories of him, because they certainly didn't have good memories of their father. It was no wonder they didn't appear to miss him. As awful as it sounded, she didn't miss him, either.

From beside the house, the gate creaked. Boffo sat, with every muscle wiggling, but controlling himself to stay as he'd been taught. Ashley held the gate open for Brendan, who walked into the yard with his arms loaded with wood and his tools slotted into a pocketed belt slung loosely around his waist. Once inside the yard, Brendan deposited everything on the ground. Matthew hustled to transport the boards, one piece at a time, to the growing pile that would be their new fence, while Brendan went back to his truck for more. Ashley dutifully opened the gate for Brendan as he went in and out.

As she'd done so many times, Shanna stopped her work to simply watch. The children were eager to help, and Brendan was always obliging to give them something to do, even though most of the time she was sure that he could have done it faster without them.

The gate banged shut for the last time, so Brendan called Boffo to come. He praised the dog well for his good behavior, giving him hugs and pats and a large dog biscuit—the largest Shanna had ever seen. It was so big that both Ashley and Matthew stared at it with their mouths open. Brendan simply grinned, obviously very pleased with himself.

Before Boffo left with his new treat, Brendan again commanded Boffo to sit. He clipped the dog chain to

Boffo's collar, then secured the other end to the nearest leg of the playscape.

They all walked to the pile of tools, where he handed Matthew and Ashley each a small hammer. Together, they started with the first section of fence and began to take it apart. Brendan had promised Shanna that, because of the dog, he would replace one section at a time. That way, by the time he left at the end of the day, there would be no openings for Boffo to escape through before he returned the next morning.

When the first section was half down, the doorbell rang. Shanna checked the time, thinking it was a good thing that the UPS driver was early today. She hurried to the door, but when she opened it, it wasn't the UPS driver.

Ray and his wife, Evelyn, stood side by side. Ray wore his usual jeans and stained white T-shirt with his leather vest, looking like an extra in a gang movie, except that this image was very real.

Evelyn looked every bit as rough around the edges as Ray. Instead of her typical skintight jeans, today she wore a skirt so short that Shanna didn't know how she could walk without exposing herself. Evelyn's makeup was about three layers too thick, and her hair was a different color than the last time Shanna saw her—it was bleached blond instead of Goth black. Shanna wondered how much more Evelyn's hair could take before it started to fall out.

Ray glared at Shanna and held out a large envelope. "I brought the papers. Sign them."

Shanna's gut tightened. "I've told you a hundred times, Ray, I'm not giving you the car. You may have helped Roger keep it running, but I'm the one who made the payments."

His eyes narrowed. "You know how many hours I spent working on that car. I'm the one who made it what it's worth. You know you owe me more than you could get for it if you sold it."

Evelyn stiffened and jutted her chin forward. "Yeah. Mechanics is worth like $95 an hour to fix a car and make it run like that."

Shanna gritted her teeth. "No." It was an old car and not worth half of what Ray claimed. But it ran well, and even if she sold it for what it was worth, at that price she could never buy another car in the same good condition.

With Evelyn beside him, Ray puffed out his chest and set his shoulders back, making them appear wider and him bigger, in general. His expression tightened, and he stepped forward.

Shanna's breath caught. This was exactly the same thing Roger had done when she made him angry. Next, he would use what he called "just a bit" of force to change her mind.

Time seemed to stand still as Ray flexed his shoulder.

Outside, in full view of the neighborhood, she was safe. But inside, where there were no witnesses, she would never win.

Ray was standing so close that she wouldn't have enough time to turn around, dash inside, and close, then lock the door.

Before Ray could think about what she was doing, Shanna shuffled one step backward, reached behind her, flicked the lock, and closed the door behind her. It wasn't the dead bolt, which could be activated only from the inside; but it was enough so that the door couldn't be opened without considerable force and, most important, noise.

"What are you doing?" he ground out between his teeth.

"I want to talk here—outside." Shanna tried to gather her courage, but she was already shaking inside. "You didn't fix the car with Roger to make money by selling it. You did it because he supplied the beer."

"Some of the money Roger used to buy the car he traded in was mine, so I have a personal interest in this one. Now I want my investment back."

"He had that old, junky car before we were married. He never told me he owed you any money for it."

He stepped forward again, backing Shanna against the locked door. She cringed, wondering whether Brendan would be able to hear her over the banging and hammering if she screamed, since none of her neighbors appeared to be outside.

Ray raised the envelope. With nowhere for Shanna to go, he pressed the corner of it to her chest. "That isn't my fault. I just want what's mine. So between what Roger owed me and all my work, I want Roger's car."

She wanted to sound forceful, but her voice came out in a squeak. "I made all the payments on it, not Roger. It's my car. Roger never told me he owed you money, and that old car wasn't worth anything, anyway. They hardly gave him anything for it."

He grabbed her arm, squeezing tight enough to make her wince. He gave her a shake. "This is the arm you broke on your little fall down the stairs. Wouldn't it be too bad if you fell and broke it again?"

Her eyes began to burn, but she fought to keep herself under control. "You can't threaten me. No one can threaten me anymore."

"I'm not threatening you. I'm talking some sense into you. I want what's owed to me."

Shanna's heart pounded, and she hoped she didn't faint. She'd thought these times were behind her. "I'm not giving you Roger's car. And if you threaten me again, I'll—I'll call the police," she choked out.

"You won't do that." His lips curled into an evil sneer, and he squeezed her arm tighter until the pain made her breath catch. She wondered how much force it would take to rebreak the same place in her arm. His voice lowered in pitch so even Evelyn wouldn't have been able to hear him. "Kids have accidents all the time. You fell down the stairs last year. Your kids might, too, and no one would question it."

Shanna's head began to spin. Like so many other women trapped in an abusive marriage, she'd foolishly told the staff at the hospital that she'd fallen. They'd known Roger had pushed her, because she'd had a black eye that night, too, as well as other bruises that happened before her alleged fall. But on the way to the hospital, he'd said he was sorry and promised it would never happen again—that he'd treat her right and he'd change.

The only things that changed were that he started drinking more and had an affair.

Shanna didn't know if Ray was cheating on Evelyn, but she had seen bruises that Evelyn had tried to conceal with too much makeup. She knew he was equally capable of doing the same to her. She could protect herself when his anger flared like this by staying where there was at least one adult witness, not including Evelyn.

But Matthew and Ashley would never think that way. They didn't like Ray, but they trusted him because he was their uncle. They were still too innocent to imagine the horrible things Ray could do to them. They wouldn't see harm coming, and they wouldn't know how to escape before it was too late.

For herself, it was one thing to report Ray to the police if he hurt or injured her. But it was different for her children. She couldn't allow him to hurt them in any way, but there was no way to protect them 24/7. She couldn't count on the police, because there was nothing they could do until after it happened. Then all they could do was arrest him, which didn't protect them from harm; that only meant that Ray would be punished after he'd done it.

She couldn't file for a restraining order, because Ray didn't have a criminal record, and Evelyn would never tell the truth about what happened in the privacy of their home.

He released her with a shove. "I'll be back tomorrow. And I don't want that guy who was here last week involved. This is between you and me."

Ray turned and strode to his pickup with Evelyn behind him, trying to keep up in her too-high spike heels.

As soon as the truck doors closed, all the adrenaline seeped out of Shanna. First her teeth started chattering; then her hands started shaking. It quickly rippled into a cascading effect until she was trembling all over.

She had to sit down before she fell down.

On shaky legs, she hurried around the side of the house and through the gate. When the gate banged shut behind her, the hammering stopped. That meant Brendan, Matthew, and Ashley were watching her and wondering why she was coming from the front, but she couldn't stop to talk. She had to think—to figure out what to do. Roger had made her life into a nightmare. She couldn't allow Ray to do the same thing.

"Mommy?" Ashley called out. "Where are you going?"

"I accidentally locked myself out," she replied over her shoulder, then ran the rest of the way to the entrance to her office. Once inside, she dropped into her chair. Resting her elbows on her knees, she lowered her face into her palms just because she couldn't keep herself straight anymore. Silent tears flowed down her cheeks, and she couldn't stop them.

The banging and hammering didn't resume. Instead, she heard Brendan's voice, muted through the wall. "You guys stay here and keep working. I want you to put all those boards in piles for me, eighteen boards to a pile. I'll be right back."

The door creaked open, and Brendan stepped inside. "Shanna? I was wondering if—what's wrong? Are you hurt?"

Her arm throbbed, but that was the least of her worries. She shook her head, not removing her hands from her face.

The metal wheels of her visitor's chair glided across the room; then the chair creaked as Brendan's weight sank onto the seat. Shanna peeked from between her fingers to see Brendan sitting directly in front of her, leaning forward, his elbows on his knees.

When he spoke again, his voice was low and firm. "Please tell me what happened."

Not caring about her blotchy face or her red eyes, she raised her head, looked straight at Brendan, and let out a ragged sigh. "It's Ray" was all she could say.

seven

Brendan's heart sank to the soles of his rubber boots.

He'd been telling himself since he started this job that he didn't want to get involved with Shanna and her little family, but with each passing day, he was grounding himself deeper and deeper into their lives. Now, even his mother was involved. And with Ray back in the picture, there was real trouble. He couldn't step back.

Brendan didn't trust Ray from the first moment he saw the man, and his gut feelings were right. He didn't know what was wrong, but he wanted to protect Shanna and her children from whatever troubles her brother-in-law wrought.

"What's the problem?"

Shanna drew in a shaky breath. His heart clenched into a little knot. "It's complicated. I'm not sure I even understand it myself."

"Is there anything I can do to help?" The words were out before he thought about what he was offering, but that didn't mean he wasn't sincere about his offer.

She looked up at him, her eyes wide and glassy.

"There's nothing you can do. Ray says that Roger owed him money that I didn't know about. He's come up with a crazy notion that between the money and work he did on Roger's car, that I owe him the car."

"Do you think it's true?"

"No. Even if Ray did give Roger money, it was before we

90

were married, and it only would have been a few hundred dollars. Nothing near the value of the car I have now. I don't believe him, anyway, and he can't prove it. I know Ray and Roger did a lot of work on the car, but there wasn't anything really wrong with it. They just liked to polish off a case of beer while they tinkered with it. Most of what they did wasn't really fixing anything."

"Then it shouldn't be an issue."

She shook her head. "Ray is a lot like Roger. He thinks everyone owes him something, including me. He figures that if he can scare me enough, I'll give him what he wants, but I can't. I only have Roger's car, and I can't afford to make payments on another one. The night Roger died, I think he knew he shouldn't have been driving. He took my car when he drank, just in case he had an accident; so it was my car he would have damaged, not his own. He just didn't expect to die in it. Insurance didn't cover it because he was well over the legal blood-alcohol limit, so now the only car I have is Roger's car. I wish I could sell it and buy something else, but it does run well, and I'd never get something this good with the money I could get for it."

"I still don't understand why he would do this."

"I heard from my mother-in-law that Ray had another accident with Evelyn's car. Just like Roger, it was while he was drinking, so their insurance won't cover the repairs. So Evelyn needs another car." She drew in another shaky breath. "I told Ray he couldn't threaten me anymore, so he threatened to hurt Matthew and Ashley."

A wave of cold dread passed through Brendan. After his first encounter with Ray, Brendan didn't doubt for a minute that Ray would hurt Shanna. From what the children had said about their father, Shanna had been in an abusive marriage. He knew that such things often cycled in families, and he suspected that the two brothers were very similar, including how they treated their wives. But as bad as that was, he couldn't imagine an adult who would deliberately harm innocent children. Yet at the same time, he read the newspapers, and he knew that happened, too.

"That's pretty serious. I think you should call the police."

"It won't make any difference. I've been through this before. Until something happens, there's nothing they can do, because Ray doesn't have a criminal record and no complaints have been filed against him. That's what makes this so frightening. I'd almost think of giving him the car and doing without if it would make him go away, but then it would just fuel him. He'd demand more, and there'd be no end to it. We'll never be safe."

Now Brendan really wanted to do something, but he didn't know what.

As if the thought struck them at the same time, they both looked into the yard to watch Matthew and Ashley. They had abandoned their task of counting the fence boards and were happily climbing the playscape.

Today they were safe. But how long would it last?

He turned to Shanna. "There has to be something that can be done to protect you. This is beyond just bullying. He can't threaten you and the kids like this and get away with it."

"He can. This kind of thing happens all the time."

"What would stop him?"

"Nothing stopped Roger except a fight he knew he couldn't win. Ray would be the same. He's bigger and stronger than me, and he knows I couldn't defend myself against him. Getting the police involved the next day doesn't scare him, because he's always been able to talk his way out of it. Roger always did, and like a fool, I went along with him, thinking it would hold the family together."

A fight he couldn't win.

The words echoed through Brendan's head.

God, between You and me, help me show Ray that he can't win this, that there is Someone greater than him out there and that You're in charge of the bigger picture.

Shanna's eyes glazed over. "He'll be back tomorrow, probably about the same time."

"Why do you say that?"

She stared out the window, her eyes unfocused. "Ray works afternoon shift at the mill, so he doesn't get out of bed until noon. He has to be back at work by 4:00, so he's limited to those hours. He never comes on the weekend, because more people are out and about, and he doesn't want any witnesses."

Brendan's stomach tightened at the thought of why Ray didn't like witnesses around when he visited Shanna.

She turned to Brendan, making direct eye contact. Her voice dropped to barely above a whisper. "I don't know why I'm telling you this. But I'm so scared."

He wanted to tell her not to be scared, but she had good reasons to be.

Brendan reached out to hold her hand, but she backed up, not allowing him to touch her.

It broke his heart to see her so nervous. "Please try not to worry. I have an idea, but I have to think about it some more."

A silence hung between them, the air thick with tension.

"Before I forget, the reason I came in here in the first place was to tell you that I've got some leftover shingles from the playscape, so I was thinking of building a doghouse."

"What do shingles have to do with a doghouse?"

Brendan stroked his beard, then crossed his arms over his chest. "It would match the house and the playscape. Don't you think the three coordinated structures would look spectacular?"

"I don't think Boffo would care."

"No, but I would." He didn't know why; he wondered if he was going soft. He had never been much of an animal lover, but now that he was spending so much time around Boffo, he was growing fond of the goofy dog. When his job with Shanna was over, he'd even miss the crazy animal. "Maybe he needs someplace to go when he knows he's in the doghouse."

She didn't smile, telling him that his pathetic attempt at humor had fallen flat. Considering what she was dealing with, he couldn't blame her.

He stood. "I need to get back to work. Call me if you need me. Let me give you my cell number." He watched as she punched his number into her auto dial. As he walked into her yard, Brendan made a mental note to set up a special ring tone on his own phone for calls from Shanna's number.

The children frolicked happily on their new playscape for the rest of the afternoon, which was both a blessing and a relief. It allowed him to put together a plan, but it was a plan for which he couldn't predict an ending. Ray didn't listen to reason or play fair.

Not that this was a game. He'd never encountered a situation more serious.

Before Brendan returned to his task, he closed his eyes and prayed for wisdom, strength, and the discernment to do what was right in God's sight.

&

Shanna heard Ray's truck before she actually saw it.

Without looking down the street to make sure, she hit the auto dial on her cell to get Brendan. He told her that he was already on the way and to stall for time.

Easier said than done.

She should have had the courage to face Ray herself, but she didn't.

She prayed that God would somehow protect her and her children, because she knew she couldn't protect herself. She'd wanted Brendan to be there to protect her, but he wasn't. She wanted to trust him, but deep inside, she still wasn't sure she could.

On the outside, Brendan seemed to be a nice man. He attended church, and according to Pastor Harry, Brendan was committed to serving his Savior. But like any man, Brendan wasn't perfect, as much as she wanted him to be.

For now, he said he wanted to protect her.

Roger had also been protective, but it wasn't long before he'd turned from merely protective to possessive. He wanted to know where she was and who she was with every minute, whether he was home or not. Toward the end, he flew into a rage if she talked to any man. When she started attending church, he didn't even trust her talking to the men there, even though most were married and with their wives.

She couldn't be sure that Brendan wouldn't also become

overly possessive and distrusting like Roger. It could be a sign of worse to come, and she couldn't go through that again. And the fact that Brendan made Ray nervous told her a lot. Ray dealt mostly with unsavory characters, so when Brendan was able to put a little fear into Ray, that made *her* nervous.

Shanna peeked through the blinds and watched Ray park his truck. Her blood turned to ice in her veins to see that today Ray was alone.

Where was Brendan?

Part of her said not to answer the door right away, to stall for time. Yet the longer she made Ray wait, the angrier he would become, and the situation would turn more dangerous than it already was.

She told Matthew and Ashley to go into the backyard to play in the fort, which suited them fine. They didn't want to see Ray any more than she did.

Shanna ran into the bathroom and listened. When the doorbell rang, she flushed the toilet, then yelled, "Just a minute!" to give herself some more time and to make Ray think it was understandable. She waited a few seconds and washed her hands to dispel the urge to phone Brendan. She expected that he was one of the few diligent drivers who would pull off the road and stop before answering his cell phone, so a phone call asking him to hurry would cause him to take even longer to arrive.

She walked down the stairs at a normal pace, knowing Ray would be watching through the window beside the door.

Just as she'd done the last time, she opened the door and stepped quickly outside, meaning to close the door behind her so they would stay in full view of the neighborhood.

Before she could grab the doorknob, Ray raised one hand and pushed so hard and fast on her left shoulder that the force caused her to stagger backward. Before she could regain her balance, Ray strode in and closed the door behind him.

In addition to the throbbing in her shoulder, hearing the click of the lock nearly caused her to throw up.

"Have you made up your mind?" he barked. "Of course you know there's only one answer."

"N—no," she muttered.

Ray's voice rose, and he stepped closer, backing Shanna against the wall. "I didn't hear the right answer!"

"You can't have the car. I don't believe that you gave Roger any money. And most of the time you guys weren't really working on the car; you were just tinkering. I don't owe you anything, especially not the car."

Ray stepped so close that their bodies almost touched, even though she flattened her back against the wall. He lifted one hand and pressed his palm on the wall beside her ear. "I must not have heard you properly. Would you like to repeat that?"

She forced herself to breathe. His hand was only inches from her throat. She had no chance of escape. She told herself to be rational—he wouldn't strangle her to death, because then she wouldn't be able to sign over the car. He was only trying to frighten her, and it was working. She couldn't remember ever being so scared, not even in the seconds before Roger pushed her down the stairs.

Shanna gulped for air. "I—I said no."

Ray's fingers brushed her neck. "Then maybe—"

A male voice sounded from the entrance to the utility

room, cutting off Ray's words. "I wouldn't do that if I were you."

A man stepped into view. A big man.

Shanna pressed herself even more into the wall. Her heart pounded. She didn't know how or why this stranger had come into her house. If he were a burglar, he didn't have her television under his arm, even though he looked big and strong enough to carry it easily.

Echoes of Matthew and Ashley laughing in the backyard sounded through the house. At least they were safe from this criminal who had somehow snuck inside.

She stared at him, struggling not to scream and show her fear.

This man could have been a pro wrestler. His worn, black T-shirt molded huge, well-defined pecs, a washboard stomach, and a trim waist. The sleeves were ripped off the shirt, probably because they couldn't stand the strain of surrounding his upper arms—which were huge and bulging with well-shaped muscles. Tight jeans showed off the most muscular pair of male legs she'd ever seen. On his feet were scuffed cowboy boots—very large cowboy boots, but then a man so tall had to have feet to support his height.

She looked up. Way up.

He wasn't movie-star handsome, but he was still quite good-looking. His dark blond hair was cut short on the sides and spiked up on top for a rough, trendy look, not the style of a business executive. He had full lips, which she'd never thought of as being attractive on a man, but on him they looked good. She couldn't make out the exact color of his eyes from across the foyer, but they were light, so they weren't brown. He narrowed those mesmerizing eyes and gritted his teeth, which accented the lines of his very masculine square jaw and high cheekbones. With the tightening in his expression, his nostrils flared slightly, drawing her attention to a nose that was a little too big for his face but added to his appeal.

The nose. . .long and accented with a rounded hump in the middle.

She'd seen that nose before.

Her heart pounded. "Brendan?" She gulped.

His tight expression relaxed, and he smiled. His eyes sparkled. "Hey, babe." His voice came out low and husky. Flirty. And possessive. "You okay?"

A flock of butterflies went wild inside her stomach. Her voice wouldn't work. She didn't know whether to shake her head or nod.

He stepped toward her, causing Ray to back up. Brendan stepped between them, then brushed her cheek with the side of his thumb. The small movement flexed the muscles in his arm.

While he was still touching her, he turned his head toward Ray. The harsh tone of his voice contrasted vividly with his gentle touch. "I don't believe you were invited."

Ray backed up another step but didn't leave. "I've got business with Shanna."

"Then that makes it my business, too. Got a problem with that?" Brendan's eyes narrowed.

Ray backed up again. One hand went behind him to the door handle. His eyes widened slightly when he realized it was locked, even though he was the one who had locked it.

One corner of Brendan's mouth tipped up and one eyebrow quirked. He flexed the muscles in his arms, and his voice lowered in pitch. "I know where you live," he said.

Ray spun around and turned the lock button. "This isn't over," he said as he stomped out.

Brendan moved so fast Shanna's hair moved with the air current. He opened the door and stepped in the doorway, standing prominently with his arms crossed over his massive chest, making his presence known to Ray and anyone who cared to watch.

Shanna watched him from behind. This new Brendan looked mighty fine, even from the back. Fit and trim and confident—as if he knew how good he looked and wasn't afraid to show it. The top of his spiked hair brushed the wooden edge of the doorframe, and his shoulders didn't have far to go on either side.

"You know, Ray," he shouted, "you're wrong. It's over because *I* think it's over."

Ray hopped into his truck and drove away with a squeal of rubber.

Brendan turned around to face her, then stepped forward, closing the door behind him. "I hope that makes him think twice."

All she could do was stare. If she could turn the clock back ten years, he was everything she would have looked for in a man in her younger days. He was the epitome of tall, dark, and handsome, except that he was blond. In addition to his good looks and obvious strength, he knew how to get what he wanted, and he followed through. Knowing him as she did, she knew that he was also ambitious and goal oriented, intelligent, and a hard worker.

Ten years ago she could have fallen in love with him. But now she knew what could happen. Now, older and wiser, she wanted a short, dignified, gentle, nearsighted accountant. Brendan wasn't an accountant. He wasn't even good with numbers. His boxes of business documents proved that.

He waited for her to say something, but no words would come.

He gave a short laugh and rubbed his chin with his thumb and index finger. "I found out this morning that I'm just as ugly as I was eight years ago."

She wanted to reassure him that he was far from ugly, but her mouth didn't work.

He lifted his hand and ran his palm along the tips of his spiked up hair. "You wouldn't believe how much gel it took to do this. The woman at the salon assured me that it would all wash out easily, but I'm not so sure I believe her. Do you know how stiff this is?"

The short hair and the shaved face suited him. It suited him too much.

"Why did you do that?" she asked when she could finally find her voice.

"I'm not really sure. I thought I'd look a little more convincing if I didn't look like just the gardener, but when I changed into my old clothes, my hair looked too sedate. So I went to get a haircut. The lady suggested that my new haircut would look better without the beard, so off it went."

His expression told her that he really didn't know how appealing he was, both clean-shaven and dressed as he was—or how tempting. If it were anyone but her looking at him.

"It suits you. I don't understand why you cover your face with that beard." Not that it was an ugly beard. It was always short and well trimmed. But it was always there.

He rubbed his chin again, the movement of his fingers causing the muscles in his arm to ripple. "It grows too fast. My five o'clock shadow begins at two. If I have to go anywhere in the evening, I have to shave twice. It was easier to just let it grow. I trim it once a week. It's easier that way."

She couldn't imagine shaving her legs twice a day. Sometimes she didn't even shave twice a week.

She continued to stare at him. In addition to the new haircut and missing beard, the clothes had changed his appearance. She knew he'd be muscular, but reality far exceeded what she'd imagined hidden beneath the loose flannel shirts he always wore.

Likewise, the baggy green work pants completely camouflaged everything his jeans showed off.

Even the cowboy boots looked good compared to his usual rubber boots.

"Thanks for stepping in like that. I hope this makes him think twice before he comes again."

"I hope so, too. But I have a feeling he's going to need to see more of me—and us together—to make him think that he's not going to be able to talk to you without going through me first."

"Excuse me?"

Brendan slid his hands down his sides, like he was going to slide his hands into his pockets, but his pants were too tight for that. He stiffened, then crossed his arms over his chest. "So far, no one has seen us together. I've been doing a lot of thinking since we last talked. To give this relationship more strength, we should be seen together in public, in places where Ray or his friends will see us and then tell him you're no longer alone."

"I'm not going to the bar."

"I didn't mean places like that. I was kind of thinking of big, public places. Places where lots of people go, from all walks of life. Certainly he has friends who have families, friends who would report back to him if they saw us together. He's got to think that he's never going to catch you alone again, or that if he does, he'll have to answer to me for anything he does. Although I hope and pray it never comes to that, because I don't want to fight him. I just want to scare some sense into him."

"I don't know if that's possible."

Again Brendan rubbed his chin, like he couldn't believe the feel of his own bare skin on his face. "I still think it's a good idea to go out in public together. We could start out with something easy. Like on Sunday, I can go to church with you and the kids."

"Church? You're never going to see Ray or anyone Ray knows at church."

Brendan grinned. "I know. But I was thinking of another reason. I haven't seen Harry for a while. I want to see if he recognizes me with my new haircut."

She certainly hadn't recognized him. "I see you came in from the back, which was a good idea since Ray locked the front door on me. Did the kids recognize you?"

"Actually, they did. But that was because of Boffo. Boffo didn't care about the beard or my new haircut, so he greeted me right away, and the kids heard me talking to him before they actually saw me. They were surprised, but they already knew it was me by the time they actually saw me. They said they liked the new me."

That would explain why she hadn't heard any commotion, allowing Brendan to sneak into the house.

He stepped closer to her. "What do you think? Should I stay this way?"

She stared upward. She did like the change. But she didn't know why what she thought would make a difference. "I like it. Why are you asking me?"

His voice dropped to a gruff whisper. "I don't know." He reached forward again, cupping her cheek with his palm. His hand was rough and calloused. The hand of a workingman.

It had been a long time since a man had been so gentle with her. She couldn't help herself. Shanna closed her eyes and leaned into his hand.

She hadn't wanted to enjoy his touch, but she did. He made her crave what she had never had—someone who valued her and treated her gently and with respect, someone who, when there was no work to do and no pressing needs to fill, would relax with her and help shut out the problems of life for a while. She craved it more than anything, but she knew she couldn't have it—at least not with Brendan. His gentleness now only served to remind her how strong he really was and how quickly the situation could turn around, if that was the way he wanted it to be.

For now it was good, but she knew things could turn very nasty. She'd lived that way for too many years. When the day came that God chose for her to marry again, He would send her that quiet accountant she'd been dreaming of.

But for now, she couldn't help herself. She was attracted to Brendan, and that was wrong. Just like the books said, she was falling into the same predictable cycles, only she could now realize it and break the cycle.

Since she knew she was falling back into it, she obviously needed another self-help book for victims of abuse, only this time Roger wasn't going to be around to threaten her for daring to read it. This time she could read it at her leisure and reread the parts she needed the most, which was to learn why she was falling into the same trap.

Brendan's movement as he shuffled closer snapped her to attention. She opened her eyes and looked up just as his eyes closed and he lowered his mouth to hers. She was too shocked to resist.

His kiss was gentle and sweet, and she found herself drifting into him. She closed her eyes and allowed herself to enjoy the experience. It felt as if she were dreaming, but this was too good not to be real.

Slowly, he broke away, but instead of stepping back, his hand dropped to her shoulder. Using his other hand, he tipped her face up with one finger under her chin. "I was worried about you. When I saw Ray was already here and the door was closed, I thought I was too late. Are you sure you're okay?"

She nodded, but when his other hand drifted to the shoulder Ray had shoved, she winced.

He jerked his hand up.

She blinked back a tear.

His eyes narrowed. "What's wrong? Don't lie to me. Did he hit you?"

"No. He only pushed me out of the way so he could close the door."

"Let me see."

She lifted her hand to shield herself from him, then

winced at her own touch.

"That looks like it hurts. I want you to show me."

"No!" If it were just her arm, it would have been easy to simply roll up her sleeve. She wasn't going to unbutton her blouse and show him where it hurt. That was much too personal.

He pulled out his cell phone and pushed one of the buttons in his auto dial.

"Who are you calling?"

"My mother. She's not working today. If it hurts that bad, he did more than just push you out of the way. I don't know why you want to protect him. If he hit you, say so. By hiding what he's done, you're protecting him and only hurting yourself. We're going to leave the kids with my mother, and I'm taking you to the clinic so this can be documented."

One of the chapters of one of the self-help books flashed before her eyes.

Brendan was right. Ray would say he only "shoved" her, but by shoving her so hard, Ray really had hurt her. By any other name, he had hit her. She couldn't allow it to continue, or she was going to make everything even worse.

"Okay. I'll go. But don't you have a job to go to?"

He punched a text message into the phone and hit SEND. "Not anymore. Get your purse. The second my mother gets here, we're gone."

eight

Brendan leaned forward, toward the mirror, checking to be sure he hadn't missed a spot. He'd been shaving for only a few days, and he could already list all the reasons he hadn't missed it for the past eight years. But today was the big day. It was Sunday morning, and even though he'd miss all his friends at his own church, today he was going to Shanna's church where he would see his friend Harry, whom he hadn't seen for a few weeks.

He grinned at the clean-shaven stranger in the mirror. Out of respect, he had to remember to address his friend with the official title of *pastor* in front of members of Harry's congregation, even though he'd known Harry since high school, years before Harry chose his path and entered Bible school, then gone on to seminary to get his master of divinity.

Today he would see if his friend recognized him in the crowd, although Harry's church—or rather, Pastor Harry's church—was fairly small. The congregation was approximately 250 people, a friendly size, but not one that had room for a lot of programs and special needs groups. His own church was huge. They had three services, all of which were packed; and outside of Sunday services, they had singles groups, over-sixty-five groups, athletic interest groups, single-parent groups, three different youth groups, college and career groups, women's and craft groups—

anything a person might want to do could be done with a group of other believers.

Brendan's smile dropped. One group he would have wanted to know about was a women's abuse group for Shanna, or at least a counselor. Even though physical violence was against God's will within a marriage, it still happened within the Christian community. Despite his involvement, knowledge and information about groups that could help her would be unavailable to men for obvious reasons.

He turned away from the mirror and returned to his bedroom to get dressed.

What was his involvement with Shanna? As a Christian brother he wanted to help her, but where did the desire simply to help another believer end?

The nurse at the clinic had shooed him out of the examination room in order to assess Shanna's shoulder, but the amount of time he was made to wait in the lobby took much longer than the time it would take to check for injury, even more than simple bruising. On the way home, Shanna had been very quiet, and she'd refused to look at him. He'd also thought a few times that she was crying, but she didn't give him the chance to see much of her face while he was driving.

When he'd taken her home, his mother was upstairs with the children in the living room. Even knowing his mother could walk in on them anytime, he'd still wanted to embrace Shanna and tell her that she was strong and everything would be okay, but she wouldn't let him touch her. The sinking feeling in his heart was more than disappointment at not being able to hug a friend. He'd felt the sting of rejection over something that wasn't his fault, and he wanted to make it right.

Brendan didn't know how much longer his mother had stayed at Shanna's house after he left, but he knew she would never tell him what he wanted to know.

He'd been at Shanna's house every day since then, working on her fence. To make the project last longer, he'd taken part of the playscape apart to make it bigger and better. Yet she never asked him what he was doing.

She was avoiding him, and he wanted to know why.

If she was afraid of him because of how the other men in her life treated her, he wanted to march over to Ray's house and give Ray a taste of his own medicine.

Brendan squeezed his eyes shut. What he was thinking was wrong. It wasn't his job to serve justice or to be judge and jury over Ray. It was his job as a Christian brother to protect Shanna and to help her overcome what Ray, and probably her husband, had done to her over the years. If Brendan threatened Ray physically to win the battle, that would make him no better than Ray. Brendan didn't want to lower himself to that level, even though it was very tempting. The right thing was to suggest that Ray go for counseling, even though Brendan knew that Ray would never do it.

Once he'd buttoned his shirt and tucked it in, Brendan stood still, more aware of his own size than he'd been for years. He was six feet five inches tall in his stocking feet, and the last time he'd stepped on the scale, he was 260 pounds, none of it fat. Yet as large as he was, when he'd arrived at Shanna's house in the clothes that showed off his physical attributes to the best advantage, he'd seen a glimmer of interest in her eyes. Then, less than an hour later, she was frightened of him.

It didn't make sense.

But that didn't matter right now. What mattered was that it was time to leave to pick up Shanna and her children and escort them to God's house of worship. For an hour and a half, within the walls of the church building, she would be safe from the troubles of the world and could soak in the warmth of God's love without worry.

❧

Shanna pasted yet another smile on her face as she introduced Brendan to another interested couple. She'd suspected that they would attract attention, but she'd never thought it would be like this. She could just imagine the chatter of the next week—that she had come to church with a man.

Not only was Brendan completely relaxed in the church crowd, but he was also perfectly sociable, happily chatting with everyone who wanted to meet him, which was most of the people there.

To make the picture more interesting to onlookers, instead of running around before the service like they usually did, Ashley stayed glued to Brendan's hand, and Matthew wouldn't leave Brendan's other side. Walking in a row—with Ashley between Shanna and Brendan—they looked like a typical, happy family unit, except that the male member of this family happened to be the Jolly Green Giant.

Shanna tried to banish the picture from her mind. Without a doubt, Brendan was the tallest person in the room, which probably wasn't unusual for him. She wondered if he'd thought about his choice of wearing a green shirt that morning.

She didn't have to turn to look at him to know how good he looked. She liked his shaved chin, and the new haircut suited him. He made her laugh countless times, complaining about the gel he had to use to keep it spiked up. He looked positively dashing in the green shirt, despite the connection of the color to his height, along with pressed black slacks, black shoes, and a black tie. Not a lot of imagination there with the color coordination, but it looked great on him. She also wondered if he kept his wardrobe basic because he had a difficult time buying clothes so big.

Brendan automatically seated them in the back row, something she'd never done, but his consideration of anyone who might have to sit behind him impressed her.

He knew all the songs and sang with enthusiasm. When the children were called to go into Sunday school, he wasn't shy when Ashley gave him a big hug—he hugged her back without hesitation or reserve before she scurried out of the room with the rest of the children.

Watching it happen almost brought tears to Shanna's eyes. Her children were more responsive to the landscaper than they were with their own father. And he responded as if it were normal.

It was difficult not to be jealous of her children's ability to be so open and trusting. She wanted to be the same way. For the first time in her life, she'd met a man who didn't judge her or insult her for being stupid, and he made her feel valued as a person. She wanted to be hugged the same way as her daughter; yet as soon as Brendan came within two feet of her, she couldn't control the gut-wrenching terror that the fantasy was over and it was payback time.

She felt the movement of Brendan beside her, accented because of her heightened awareness of him *and* his size. He leaned down to whisper in her ear.

"Harry, er, Pastor Harry is a good speaker, isn't he?"

"Yes. He is."

Brendan snickered. "When he was still in college, whenever our senior pastor let him speak for a Sunday service, I used to sit in the front row and do everything I could to distract him. I keep telling him that's why he's such a good speaker. Because of me. It keeps him humble."

"Shh! He's about to start. Pay attention!" she whispered without turning her head.

As Pastor Harry shared his sermon, not only did Brendan pay strict attention, but he wrote notes in both his bulletin and in a very worn Bible, already full of notes in many different colors of ink.

Shanna forced herself to breathe. How could she think that Brendan was the least little bit threatening? He'd gone to church all his life, and his best friend was a pastor. His Bible was well-read and full of notes, obviously used often—probably every day. Her children loved him. Even her dog loved him. She didn't know what was wrong with her that she couldn't do the same.

"Shanna? Are you okay?"

She looked up at him. Even though they were both sitting, he was still big. "I'm fine," she muttered. "I was just thinking of something."

Before she realized what he was doing, he reached down and picked up her hand. He twined their fingers together, gently closed his fingers over her hand, then patted their joined hands with his other hand. "Everything will be fine. I promise."

He smiled, straightened, then settled back into his chair, except he didn't release her hand.

Her first impulse was to pull away, but before she actually did, she realized that he was holding her hand without any pressure—he was allowing her to pull her hand out without resistance if that was what she wanted.

That wasn't what she wanted.

He was giving her a choice, and she chose to keep things as they were.

Her heart raced, and her cheeks grew warm.

She wondered if this was how the teens felt holding hands in church.

It was innocent yet meant so much—at least it meant a lot to Shanna. Even when they were dating, when Roger held her hand, he made it clear that they were holding hands because he wanted to, and he didn't release her hand until he was ready. Even then it was a demonstration of power. He'd just told her it was because he thought she was special.

Brendan was making it completely her choice, putting himself in a somewhat vulnerable position to be rejected if she chose to pull away. That he was willing to let her make the choice showed that he didn't need to demonstrate his power—his strength was inside, where it could be seen only if a person cared to look.

She gave his hand a little squeeze to let him know she appreciated his gesture. He smiled without turning his head, still paying attention to Pastor Harry's sermon.

Shanna sighed. If only Brendan were a foot shorter, a

hundred pounds lighter, and an accountant. And didn't wear green.

When the sermon was over, Brendan released her hand to stand and sing the last song.

All through Pastor Harry's benediction, Brendan grew restless beside her. At the closing "amen," instead of filtering to the table at the back of the room to get coffee and a doughnut before the children were dismissed, she followed Brendan to the front of the church.

Pastor Harry smiled when he saw her, although she did notice that he tried to hide his surprise that she'd come with a man.

"Shanna! It's so good to see you!" Pastor Harry extended his hand toward Brendan. "And I see you brought a friend."

Brendan's hand met his friend's, but when he spoke, he spoke with a fake accent so bad that Shanna couldn't tell what he was trying to imitate. "Reverend Harry. Shanna, she has told me so much about you."

Pastor Harry's smile faltered momentarily when Brendan didn't let go of his hand. "That's good to hear. . . ." His voice trailed off. "Do you live nearby?"

Brendan increased the speed of the handshake, and his fake accent thickened. "I come from very far away. Very, very far."

"How long will you be visiting our country? Would you and Shanna care to be our guests for lunch?"

When Brendan still didn't stop shaking his hand, Pastor Harry looked down, while Brendan replied, "Ah, yes! It would very much honor me to accept your invitation. I hear your wife, she is a fine cook. Makes good borscht but doesn't use beets."

Pastor Harry raised his head, his eyes narrowed, and he leaned forward. "Brendan?" He straightened and began to laugh. "Brendan Gafferty! What did you do to your face?" Both men laughed, released each other's hands, and embraced in a manly, back-slapping hug.

When they stepped back, Brendan was still grinning. "I hope you know that you can't take back your invitation for lunch."

Pastor Harry wiped his eyes and grinned. "I wouldn't dream of it. Noon?"

"See you there. I hope you've got good ice cream."

"Brendan!" Shanna hissed.

"Don't worry. His wife always keeps a couple of cartons of Rocky Road in the freezer. One of them has my name on it."

Before Shanna could say any more, Ashley appeared in front of Brendan, offering up the craft she'd made in Sunday school.

He hunkered down and accepted it graciously, then looked up at Shanna. "I'm sorry. I should have asked you first. I hope you don't have plans."

"I was expecting to go home, but I'll gladly accept the invitation, even though I think you took advantage of Pastor Harry."

"He had it coming. Besides, he borrowed a few of my tools that I need back. If you want to go visit with your friends, go ahead. I'm going to help clean up and stack the chairs, and then we can go."

nine

Brendan drove away from his friend's house slowly, giving Ashley and Matthew ample opportunity to wave at Harry's wife, who was standing in the window holding their little poodle-mix dog.

"I've got an idea," he said quietly, so only Shanna could hear, as he turned onto the main road. "How would you like to pick Boffo up and go for a walk around Green Lake?"

She turned and looked into the backseat. "Ashley hasn't had a nap. She'll be pretty cranky tonight, so I'm not sure."

"What if she has a short nap on the way there? Would that work?"

"She's not a baby. Do you really expect her to fall asleep with all this action going on?"

"Will she be able to sleep after she calms down if everything else is quiet? It will take about half an hour to get there from your house. I can put her booster seat in the front with me, since this truck was built before the days of passenger-seat air bags."

Shanna turned and looked over her shoulder at her children, who were in the backseat of his crew cab. "That sounds like it could work. It's such a nice day; I'll take the chance."

While he drove, Shanna told the kids what they had planned. She gently suggested that Ashley sit still and that they would only have fun if everyone was quiet enough for Ashley to have a nap.

He drove quickly to Shanna's house so they could all change into more comfortable clothes, including Brendan. He always kept some clean clothes under the seat since he often got dirty on the job.

To keep things quiet for Ashley, Shanna, Matthew, and Boffo shared the backseat of the cab, and Brendan buckled Ashley's booster seat in the front beside him. They kept the music low, and talking in the back was reduced to just above a whisper. Ashley fell asleep about five minutes after they left Shanna's house.

Being a single man, he was accustomed to his truck being silent, as he usually drove alone. Everyone was being silent for Ashley, which somehow emphasized the crowd. They could have been a family, complete with the family dog curled up and sleeping in the middle of the backseat.

It made Brendan wonder if this was what it would be like when he finally got married and had a family of his own.

Strangely, he couldn't picture anyone except for Shanna and her two kids in his truck, with maybe the addition of a baby's car seat in the middle.

Mentally, Brendan shook his head. He had his life planned out. He was going to have two—exactly two—children of his own, and a purebred golden lab. He would give his children everything he'd never had, without killing himself or ignoring his family to do it. It wasn't unreasonable, and it was realistic.

He couldn't find a parking spot at the park, but he didn't mind parking a couple of blocks away. They were already planning to walk the three miles around the lake, so another couple of blocks wouldn't make any difference.

Ashley woke up as soon as they stopped moving, which was a good thing; because the exact second Brendan turned off the engine, Boffo roared to life.

Brendan reached into the bin between the seats and pulled out the leash he always kept in the truck. "Boffo, sit," he commanded.

The dog sat, but Brendan could tell by the wiggles that Boffo's willpower wouldn't last long.

The second the clip of the leash signified that it was attached, Boffo's control ended. He practically flew into the front seat, landing squarely in Brendan's lap.

"Good job training that dog, I'd say." Shanna giggled.

Brendan mumbled his response, but inside he thought it was good to hear Shanna laugh. She didn't laugh enough. The heartwarming sound made him want to make her laugh again.

They scrambled out of the truck and walked quickly to the park. Before they started on the path, Shanna took Ashley into the public restroom.

"Is this going to be fun?" Matthew asked while they waited.

"Yes, it is. Haven't you ever been to Green Lake before?"

"No. I was sick the day my school came here for a field trip."

"Didn't your daddy ever bring you here?"

"No."

"Then where did he take you when it was just you and him?"

Brendan waited for Matthew to tell him some of the other places they'd gone, but Matthew only shrugged his shoulders, which Brendan thought unusual.

He thought of other places that would be fun for a father-son outing.

"Did your dad ever take you to Bainbridge Island?"

"I never been to no island. I can't swim good."

"You don't swim there. You go on a ferry. That's a big boat you can park your car on."

Matthew's eyes widened. "I've never been on a boat like that."

Never been on a ferry. . . Living in Seattle and never been on a ferry. It was a sad thought. He wondered what else Matthew had missed out on.

Brendan remembered the many times his mother had taken him north into Canada to go shopping when he was a boy. He didn't particularly enjoy shopping, but the adventure of crossing the border had been memorable, especially waiting in the long line of cars. Then, once they were across the border, all the speed signs were different, on the metric system. He remembered having his calculator out, and every time they passed a new sign, he figured out how fast they were supposed to be going. But then, if Roger had never taken the boy to Bainbridge Island, he doubted Roger would have taken the trouble to go as far as the border.

Brendan doubted Matthew's father would have taken him to Pike Place Market, either, so he didn't ask about that.

He knew Matthew liked to play baseball. When Brendan was little, he'd gone to the old Seattle Kingdome with his father just once before his father died. As an adult, he'd watched the news when the Kingdome was demolished, feeling as if a part of him were being chopped away, along with a part of history. But now the new stadium with the retractable roof had been constructed, and it was a major hit, given the Seattle weather. When the weather was good, it was an open-air stadium; but when it rained—and it rained often—they could close the roof. It only took ten minutes if the weather was calm, or twenty minutes at the longest if it was windy. The first time he'd been there while the roof closed, he'd been fascinated. It still fascinated him, even as an adult. "What about baseball games? Did your dad ever take you to Safeco Field to see the Mariners play?"

Finally, Matthew's eyes lit up. "We watched lots of baseball games on TV. He said it was better that way because the beer was cheaper at home."

Beer. He remembered Shanna saying that Roger had died in an alcohol-related automobile accident. It stunned him to think that sitting and drinking beer was more important to Roger than taking his son out to an action-packed ball game.

"Do you go places with your mother and your sister?"

Matthew broke out into a full smile. "Mommy took me and Ashley on the Space Needle! It was way high and real fun! Have you ever been on the Space Needle?"

Brendan smiled back. "Yes. It was fun to be so high."

Shanna's voice stopped him from asking Matthew any more questions. "We're back and ready to start our adventure. Let's go!"

Brendan held Boffo's leash and walked beside Shanna as they made their way around the park. Since he hadn't expected to do anything after church, he hadn't brought his camera, but Shanna had a small digital camera with her. She took countless pictures of the children running and playing, the lake, the ducks, and even a few of him walking with Boffo—which he couldn't understand, but he put up with it.

About halfway through their walk, the children stopped running in circles around them and started to walk more quietly beside him. By about the two-and-a-half-mile point, Brendan gave Shanna Boffo's leash so that he could carry Ashley.

When they were nearly at the end, Brendan asked, "Who wants to have supper at Spuds?"

Shanna stopped walking. "Spuds? I haven't eaten there in years. What a great idea!"

Brendan shuffled Ashley into one arm and reached for his wallet in his back pocket.

"This was my idea, so this is my treat."

"I can't let you do that. There's three of us and only one of you. Do you know how much that's going to cost?"

He didn't want to tell her that he was hungry from all the walking and would probably eat as much by himself as the three of them combined. "Never mind. This is my treat. If you want to feed me, I'll stay at your place for supper one day. I don't get many home-cooked meals."

Ashley was too tired to respond, but Matthew started tugging on his mother's arm. "Did you hear that? Mr. Brendan wants to stay at our house for supper! Can we make spaghetti?"

"I think when Mr. Brendan stays, we can make something more special than just spaghetti."

Brendan turned and headed toward the restaurant. "It's

a deal. Come on. I'm starved."

Because of the dog, they couldn't sit at a table, so he lowered Ashley onto the grass under a tree and left them all at the park. This way they could have a picnic, like several other people with dogs were doing.

He bought one-piece fish-and-chip dinners for the kids, a two-piece dinner for Shanna, and a three-piece dinner for himself—knowing he would finish what the kids didn't eat—and then joined them at the park.

They didn't talk much while they ate, but he did notice Shanna sneaking glances at him, as if she couldn't believe the amount he was eating. It almost made him not want to touch what the kids left behind, except Spuds fish and chips were too good to waste. He finished up the leftovers without guilt, even though they all stared at him. He still managed to sneak a few pieces to Boffo, who was drooling so much there was a wet spot on the grass beneath his lolling tongue.

The walk back to his truck was much more sedate than the walk to the park. He almost laughed at how quiet the return trip was.

By the time they arrived at Shanna's house, he was yawning almost as much as the children.

"They'll sleep good tonight," Shanna said, yawning herself. "This was a great idea. Thank you."

"I'll help you take them inside. I think Ashley needs to be carried."

Shanna grinned. "She doesn't *need* to be carried. But she does *like* to be carried."

"Then that's an even better reason to carry her in. I want her to have good memories of this day." *I know she never had these kinds of days with her father.* Brendan had good memories of his own father and things they'd done together. That never would happen for these kids, but he could give them memories that were second best.

Ashley leaned into him a little more with each small bounce on the steps. Even though he usually took the stairs two at a time, today he walked up one step at a time, just to make the trip last a little bit longer.

Once at the couch, he didn't want to put Ashley down, but he felt stupid just standing there holding her. Slowly and gently, he nestled Ashley into the corner against the armrest. While he settled her in, Shanna picked up the remote, and VeggieTales came alive on the screen.

With Ashley and Matthew occupied, Shanna walked down the stairs with him to the door. He tried to keep a straight face when she didn't go all the way down. She stood on the second step so she was nearly at eye level with him. Being at the same height gave him thoughts as to the possibilities.

"If you give me your e-mail address, I can send you some of the pictures I took." Shanna yawned. "When I get the energy to download the camera."

Her yawn was contagious. Brendan raised his hand to cover his wide-open mouth as he yawned, too. "That would be great. I can't believe how much energy it takes to keep track of two little kids."

"Good night, then. I'll see you tomorrow."

Instead of reaching for the door, in order to make his intentions perfectly clear, he stepped closer to Shanna. Moving very slowly, he rested his hands around her waist.

"Good night, Shanna," he said, his voice coming out

much too husky, but he couldn't do anything about it.

He wanted a good night kiss, except this time he wanted her to kiss him.

He lowered his head even closer, so she only had to lean forward the tiniest little bit and it would happen.

Her eyes lowered as she looked at his mouth. His heart began to pound and his breath came faster, even though nothing had happened except anticipation.

In slow motion, she raised one hand, then ran her fingertips along his chin, making a raspy sound against the rough growth of his two o'clock shadow.

"I like it better when you don't have the beard," she said, her voice pitched lower than usual.

His eyes drifted shut, waiting. If she didn't kiss him, he just might die.

Shanna's soft lips touched his, sending his heart into a tailspin. Her kiss was slow, gentle, and light, almost a question, until her hands rested on his shoulders. She tipped her head and kissed him more fully.

Brendan's world shifted off its axis. His hands drifted from her waist to her back, and he embraced her fully as he kissed her the way he wanted to.

Much too soon, she moved back, breaking the sweet contact, and he immediately felt the loss.

"Good night," she whispered. "I guess I'll see you tomorrow."

He let his hands drop. "Yeah. Tomorrow."

With Shanna watching him from the second stair, he turned and let himself out.

&

Shanna hit the SAVE key. Satisfied that she'd completed

another task, she allowed herself to stop working and watch what was happening in her backyard.

Again, the playscape was different than it had been the day before. Today's addition was a small deck extending out from the now two-story fort.

She had no idea why Brendan was never satisfied, but with every change, his mother faithfully painted the new section and touched up the existing structure as needed. Shanna couldn't complain. She liked Kathy, and they were becoming good friends. Kathy also never asked her how she felt about Brendan, which made Shanna extremely grateful. She didn't have an answer.

Shanna stared at the playscape, again complete, at least for the moment. Every time he allegedly finished it, it was always better than the previous version.

Besides his constant work on the playscape, Brendan now had half the fence rebuilt. He wasn't there every day, but on the days he was, he changed one or two complete sections, including new fence posts; so that by the time he left, the fence was again whole, a mix of old and new, but solid enough so the yard was again fully enclosed and Boffo couldn't escape.

She watched Boffo, who was currently running around the yard with Brendan's leather tool belt in his mouth. With aspirations higher than her ability, Ashley ran behind him, chasing the dog, never able to recover the treasure of the moment. Boffo could have run faster if he wanted to, but it seemed he purposely ran just a little faster than Ashley to keep her chasing him. For now, Brendan ignored both Boffo and Ashley while he held the level up to make sure the newest fence post was perfect.

For all his running around while Brendan was present, Boffo never once tried to make a dash through whatever section of the fence was open, even when Brendan had to leave the yard for a few minutes to get something out of his truck. Somehow, Brendan had him trained to stay in the yard, fenced or not.

Because of Brendan, Boffo was again the talk of the neighborhood, not in the same way as before, as a problem. Now everyone thought he was the smartest dog they'd ever seen.

Even though dog school was now finished and Boffo had passed all his tests, Brendan continued to work with Boffo. Instead of normal, sensible dog tricks, Brendan had moved on to teaching Boffo stupid dog tricks. Boffo would howl on command, dance, or balance a biscuit on his nose until given permission to eat it.

Boffo's favorite activity involved catapulting a tennis ball from a small mechanism Brendan had constructed. With the ball in place, Boffo pressed a button with his paw, causing the ball to shoot out for him to chase. It didn't seem to bother the dog that a person wasn't throwing the ball for him. He was quite happy to play ball by himself. Shanna thought this quite odd, but at the same time, very practical, as he was never bored.

In addition to fetching the ball, Boffo now also fetched Brendan's tools on command instead of burying them. The amazing thing was that Boffo knew the difference when Brendan called his tools by name. Boffo never failed to bring exactly what Brendan needed at that particular moment. It wouldn't have surprised Shanna if Brendan trained Boffo to hammer in nails. She couldn't believe his patience with the dog. He was even better with her children. They were going to miss him dearly when he was finished.

Shanna suddenly didn't want Brendan to finish the fence. She was going to miss him, too. Probably even more than the children would—which she didn't understand. She couldn't deny that she liked him—from a distance. But still, no matter how many self-help books she read, she couldn't control the nervousness she felt with him, even though he'd never done anything threatening or violent to her.

He'd never been anything but a perfect gentleman. He was the type of man who could have had women melting at his feet. Shanna had almost melted at his feet a couple of times. Those were the times he'd kissed her and she hadn't been nervous—she had known exactly what he was going to do, because the moment had been gentle and romantic. Probably one of the reasons he was so easy to like was because his face was an open book. One look at him told her exactly what he was thinking and what kind of mood he was in. So far, all his moods had been relatively good. In all the time she'd known him, she'd seen him annoyed but never angry—unless he really had been angry with Ray but bottled it up inside so she couldn't tell. If that were the case, it made him even more dangerous than Roger, because she would never know in advance when he was going to explode with rage. Knowing his potential, she couldn't be sure of what he would do when that moment came. All she knew was that she didn't want to be near him when it happened.

No matter how hard Shanna tried or how much she wanted to, she was too afraid to trust Brendan. It wasn't fair to him, and she'd prayed about it more times than she could count, but she couldn't make it happen.

Shanna returned her attention to her screen, since she was supposed to be working. She hadn't transferred much information when the ring of Brendan's laughter stopped her.

Outside, Boffo was wearing Ashley's pink hair bow behind one ear, enjoying the attention while Ashley hugged him. Matthew was pointing at the dog and his sister, making the sourest face Shanna had ever seen. Brendan was watching Matthew, laughing so hard he was holding his sides. The laughter made Matthew's expression turn even more sour. Matthew's disdain caused Ashley to hug Boffo even more. Boffo sat, his tongue lolling, without a care in the world, despite how pathetic and ridiculous he looked wearing Ashley's hair accessory.

The sight almost brought tears to her eyes. If Brendan was an accountant, she easily could have fallen in love with him.

Brendan tamped down his laughter to unclip his cell phone from his belt and flip it open to take a call. The mood had been broken, so Shanna returned to her work. She hadn't completed more than a few more entries into her data file when Brendan walked into the room with Boffo, who was still wearing the pink bow. When Brendan halted, Boffo stopped and sat, as he'd been trained.

Shanna smiled. "I can't believe the difference in him since dog school. I don't know how I can thank you. He does everything we tell him, and he even behaves off the leash in the baseball field."

Brendan squatted to pat Boffo, which put him below Shanna's eye level.

"Speaking of that, my friend who runs the dog school

just phoned. Every year he has a competition, and he invites the top participants from each session throughout the year to enter. The cable channel sends a crew there, and they'll air it a few days after the taping as an interest segment. After the competition, there's a banquet and prizes, and any profits are donated to the local animal shelter. That's why the cable channel is there every year. Jeff says Boffo's done really well, and he thinks Boffo could win a prize. Even if he doesn't, it's always fun. Do you want to go?"

"Are you saying that people will have their dogs at a banquet?"

He grinned. "Well, it is a dog school thing. Everyone there will have a dog at home that probably sits in the kitchen while they eat. It's just like home, except on a larger scale, and there won't be any kids."

Shanna froze. "No kids?"

"It's a competition and an adult function. I think it's best to leave them at home. I can ask my mother if she can babysit."

Shanna stared into his face, actually able to look down because Brendan was still positioned low, with Boffo. Since she'd met him, she'd acknowledged his blue eyes, but she'd never been so close to him in bright daylight. His eyes were gorgeous—a bright, slate blue that could have been the eyes of a movie-star idol. Except that Brendan wasn't a movie star. He was her landscaper and, more important, the person who was saving her from her devious brother-in-law and all his plans to take away everything she valued.

Today he was asking her to go out for dinner with him, without the children, and he was even offering to arrange for babysitting.

Dog or not, it sounded like a date. She didn't want to date him, but he'd done so much work with the dog for her, she couldn't say no.

"When is this banquet happening?"

"Tomorrow."

"I'll go under one condition."

One eyebrow quirked. "Name it."

"Don't wear green."

ten

Brendan couldn't have been prouder if Boffo had been his own dog. Boffo had been the best trained in the room, and Shanna had a new, large-sized bag of top-brand dog food to prove it. He leaned toward Shanna, who was absently scratching Boffo behind one ear.

"In the fall, when it starts up again, what do you think of signing Boffo up for agility trials?"

"What kind of trials?"

"That's the thing where the dogs jump over hurdles, go over seesaws, run through tunnels, that kind of stuff."

Her face lit up. "I've seen those on television. That looks like such fun."

"I could easily build any of those things. I figure we could pick out what would be the most fun; then we could set up a small practice track in the yard."

"We?"

He bent and patted Boffo as he spoke, purposely not looking at Shanna. "Training can be pretty intense, because the handler has to run beside the dog the whole time. It's too exhausting for one person. I figure it would take both of us to keep up with him."

He waited for her to say that she didn't want his participation, mentally arming himself with an argument for when she did.

The longer he waited, the more he felt a dark cloud

of impending doom growing over his head. When he completed his work in her yard, he would have no reason to see her again except for bimonthly visits to bring his invoicing and expense receipts. He also still worried about Ray barging in on her when there was no one to defend her. For the one day, he'd sent Ray running, but the issue hadn't concluded. He knew Ray would be back; he just didn't know when. While it was a critical concern, his reason for not wanting to stop seeing Shanna wasn't entirely to simply protect her. He needed a way to keep seeing Shanna, just for the pleasure of being with her. He didn't want to stop seeing her kids, either, or her goofy dog.

"I've been meaning to talk to you about your plans, actually."

Brendan's day just got brighter. "Really?"

"You're finished with the playscape, right? And the fence is almost done, isn't it?"

His day dimmed. "Why are you asking?"

Shanna's posture stiffened, which Brendan didn't think was a good sign. "You've done so much more than our original agreement. I'll never be able to pay you back."

"I don't want you to pay me back. You're still working on catching up my accounting stuff, aren't you?"

"Well. . .yes. . ."

"Then we're not even. I told you it would be a big job."

"But you're working on my yard more than I'm working on your stuff. I have other clients' work to do, too, so yours is just one more in the pile."

"I'm working on other projects at the same time, too. Lately, I've only been at your place in the afternoons, and not every day, and only for a few hours. Just consider it something I want to do. It's been fun building something like that with no restrictions. Think of it as when Matthew builds things out of those little plastic bricks. The fun isn't in the finished project. It's in the construction."

"That may be so, but your construction project is a lot larger and a lot more expensive than his."

Brendan shrugged his shoulders. "Maybe, maybe not. My mother still has my bin from when I was a kid. Whenever she wants something, she reminds me of the estimated cost of what it took to get that bin so full. That stuff isn't cheap."

"I'm not going to win this argument, am I?"

"Nope."

The announcement came over the intercom that the Freestyle Dog Tricks category was about to begin, thankfully allowing him to change the subject. "Wait until you see what I'm going to do."

Shanna looked down at Boffo, who was now lying on his side on the floor, sprawled out and not caring what was going on around him. "When exactly did you have time to teach him something new? You've been busy working every day, and like you said, not always at my house."

"I'm just going to use what he already knows. You'll see. We're going to get the trophy, plus we're going to be featured on the cable channel." He couldn't contain his grin. "I also have ulterior motives. If Boffo wins, then they'll give me a short interview, and I can plug both our businesses: my landscaping services and your bookkeeping. Boffo will also earn a year's worth of dog food, which, for him, is a lot of kibble."

Without waiting for her response, Brendan told Boffo to stay, not that the dog looked like he had any intention of moving, then left to get his box of supplies out of his truck. When his name was called, he put the box on one side of the stage, took out a few boards, and moved to the other side of the stage from the box.

"Boffo, come!" he called.

Shanna released Boffo from the leash. Boffo scrambled to his feet and bounded across the room to go sit at Brendan's feet.

Brendan sat on the floor with his small pile of boards. "I need your help, dog. Have you seen my hammer?"

Boffo ran to the box, picked out the hammer, and brought it to him.

Brendan pretended to search his pockets. "Oops. I forgot the nails."

Boffo returned to the box, retrieved a cloth bag, and brought it to him. Brendan pretended to act surprised. A few people in the audience snickered.

One item at a time, Brendan had Boffo retrieve everything from the box he asked for, about a dozen different tools, to show everyone what Boffo was capable of. He talked to the dog as if the dog could understand, and soon the entire room echoed with laughter while Brendan continued to pretend he was more clueless than the dog.

Once or twice, Brendan snuck a few glances at Shanna, who wasn't laughing. Every time she saw him looking at her, she rolled her eyes and shook her head, having seen it all before. However, when she'd seen him do the same thing in her backyard, it hadn't been a game. In her yard, when he was trying to work, it was a matter of self-preservation.

After making a big production out of the project of building a foot-high mini-fence, when he had a few boards nailed together, Brendan stood and looked down at it. "I don't think it's level."

Brendan held his breath. This was the one thing he hadn't had time to practice to perfection with Boffo. He'd concentrated his efforts on teaching Boffo to bring his tools, instead of running away with them, in order to get his work done. The audience didn't know it, but this last thing was the only part of the routine he'd really taught Boffo as a trick.

Boffo retrieved the level, the last item from the box. Carefully Boffo balanced it on the lengthwise piece of wood and shuffled back.

Brendan looked down and rubbed his chin, pretending to study the bubble. "I don't think it's right. What do you think?" He knew the audience wouldn't know what he was doing, but he waved one arm in the air, making it look like he was frustrated and simply talking with his hands. However, he'd worked those motions out as a hand signal for Boffo, knowing that his words weren't specific enough for Boffo to take them as a command.

Right on cue, Boffo trotted back to the level. Brendan touched his nose, so Boffo nudged the level with his nose. Brendan put one hand on the side of his head, which made Boffo turn his head as if examining the bubble. For the last signal, Brendan waved his arm to give Boffo the "bark" signal. Obediently, Boffo barked once, looked up at Brendan, and sat. Half the audience roared with laughter; the other half clapped.

"Good boy!" Brendan quickly pulled a dog biscuit out of his pocket and gave it to Boffo without making him balance it on his nose first.

The applause was thunderous. As if he knew he'd done

well, Boffo rubbed against Brendan's leg, asking for approval. Brendan couldn't control his joy; Boffo had done everything perfectly. He gave Boffo a big hug and ruffled his ears.

When the applause died down, he released Boffo and they returned to the table.

Shanna leaned toward him. "You're going to be a tough act to follow. You two are a great team."

"It's not me. You've got yourself a good dog here, Shanna."

They quieted while the other teams did their tricks, but Brendan's attention was focused mainly on the woman beside him. Since she'd mentioned it, he couldn't stop thinking of what he was going to do when he'd finished her fence and done all his imagination could allow with her playscape—or anything else in her yard. When he'd first started working for her, he had wanted the job to be finished as soon as he could get everything looking presentable. Now that he was almost done, he was stalling, making changes on things that didn't matter, just to make it last longer. It wasn't her yard or anything in her yard that was important.

Trying not to be obvious about it, while everyone else watched the dog and his master on the stage, Brendan watched Shanna. He didn't want to be limited to seeing her only for business purposes. He wanted to see her often. Every day. He wanted Shanna in his life permanently, and it had nothing to do with work. It was all personal. Very personal.

He squeezed his eyes shut. This wasn't what he'd planned. He wanted to fall in love with a woman who would openly love him back; then together they would raise a family of two kids in a house with a white picket fence. It was happening, but not in the right order. It wasn't white or a picket fence, but he was working on a fence that surrounded a house already filled with two kids and their mother—a wonderful, warmhearted Christian woman who was keeping him at the end of a long stick. Brendan didn't want to be reminded that he was almost finished with her fence and that there was nothing more he could do to the playscape without making it into a miniature house. He didn't want his time with her to be over.

He opened his eyes and stared at Shanna, who was watching a couple of Jack Russell terriers jumping through hoops. It wasn't his plan, but apparently it was God's plan, and Brendan was going to have to jump through a few hoops himself. He wanted to marry Shanna. He wanted to adopt her kids, and he wanted to have more kids after that. A whole herd of kids. Except he didn't know if she wanted more kids. He really didn't know if she wanted to get married again. Her first marriage hadn't exactly been a relationship made in heaven, and her life was still in a constant state of disruption because of it. He didn't know what to do, and time was running out.

While watching her, he prayed for God to tell him something, but the only thing that came to him was to show her that he loved her. Before he could think of anything practical, the last act ended.

She turned to him and smiled, completely destroying all his thought processes. "They were all so good! But I still think you and Boffo were the best."

"We'll see," he muttered.

The people from the next table called to them, and they shared thoughts on all the acts until the judging panel returned from their deliberation. A silence hung over the room for a few seconds, which was as long as could be expected considering the number of dogs in the room. The emcee held up a small, bone-shaped trophy for everyone to see, then announced that Boffo was the winner.

"You did it!" Shanna sang out.

"No, we did it. You were just as much a part of this."

Show her that you love her. The words chorused through his head.

He turned, leaned down, and kissed her cheek, knowing everyone in the room was watching them. Before she could respond, he stood, grabbed her hand, and pulled her to her feet. "Now let's go get that trophy. Smile for the camera."

Taking advantage of the fact that she was still flustered, he held on to her hand and led her to the front, knowing that to everyone present, they looked very much like a happy couple with their faithful dog beside them. He felt like puffing his chest out like a proud rooster.

Once at the front, while everyone watched, he stepped aside for Shanna to accept the trophy. After all, she really was Boffo's owner.

She smiled graciously and held it up to the camera as he leaned down and kissed her cheek again, knowing she couldn't do anything with the camera on them; then he whispered in her ear, "Keep smiling. It's time for everyone else to leave and for us to go get interviewed."

❧

Shanna tried to contain her excitement as she hung up the phone.

Brendan had been right. She wouldn't have thought the local cable channel had a large following, but Brendan's friend had posted advertising in every pet food store and community advertising board in the area, generating much local interest.

In front of the camera, Shanna had been too nervous to say much, but nervousness wasn't a fault of Brendan's. Not only did he tell the camera about how much his friend's dog school had helped Boffo, but when the interviewer asked about what he did when he wasn't training Boffo, he gave a short prepared presentation on both his landscaping business and Shanna's bookkeeping services.

Already, the next day, two people representing moderate-sized businesses had phoned to inquire about what she could do for them.

Just as she hung up from her call, the rumble of Brendan's truck echoed in front of her house.

She could hardly wait to tell him the good news. She stood, but instead of hearing the engine shut off, she heard it rev and the truck drive away.

Shanna sank into her chair. It wasn't that she was disappointed at being unable to share her good news. The sinking feeling was more than that.

She was disappointed that she didn't get to see Brendan, no matter what the reason.

The knowledge scared her. Being with Brendan both excited her and terrified her. Everything about him she liked, and she liked *a lot*. Probably even too much. How he could be so gentle. . . How he worked so hard and was so meticulous with his work. . . How he played with the children. . . His kindness to the dog. . . His sense of humor. . . How wonderfully he'd kissed her.

Shanna buried her face in her hands. It was what she

didn't know that scared her: How he would act when things didn't go right. . . What he would do when Ray stood up to him. . . His reaction when her opinion on something was different than his. . .

Boffo scurried to the door, breaking Shanna out of her thoughts.

As she reached to open the door, someone grasped the door handle from the outside. Whoever it was stood to the side instead of in front of the door as the knob turned. From that angle, she couldn't see the person through the small window. She could only see that it was a man's hand.

Shanna froze. She was alone and defenseless. At least the children were upstairs in their rooms, safe unless they came downstairs.

The door started to open.

Shanna screamed.

The gentle glide of the door's movement changed to an abrupt thrust, and the door was fully open in a split second.

Brendan burst inside. "Where is he?" Brendan barked as he stepped past her.

Seeing nothing, he stood still.

Shanna was shaking so badly she couldn't speak.

"Is he hiding?"

Her voice came out in a squeak, but at least she found it. "Who?"

"Ray. Isn't he here?"

"N–no," she stammered, still shaking.

"What's wrong? I heard you scream."

"I heard your truck drive away. I thought you forgot something and left."

"A friend of mine needs to move some lumber, so I let

him borrow my truck. He dropped me off, and he's going to come get me at 4:30."

"I didn't think you were coming. Then, when I saw your hand and the door opening, I thought it was Ray, sneaking in to get me, knowing I was alone. I should have known it was you when Boffo didn't bark. I'm sorry."

"You're sorry?" He stared at her; then his eyebrows rose. "Don't be sorry. I'm the one who should be sorry for frightening you." He opened his arms, and his voice lowered to a comforting rumble. "Come here."

Shanna couldn't help herself. He called and she went. The second she was there, his arms closed around her in a comforting embrace. She found the strength not to cry, but she couldn't resist sinking into his warmth.

She shouldn't have been there, but she was. Again, history had repeated itself. Roger had done it to her all the time. He'd frighten her, sometimes by shoving her while they were arguing. Sometimes he would storm up to her in such a fit of rage that she thought she'd brought him to the point where he would hit her. Sometimes just the way he shouted threats and insults at her would break her down. Then, when he'd reduced her to a quivering mess, he'd call her to him and she would go, knowing that as soon as she was in his arms it would be over and she would be safe.

It didn't make sense when he'd been the one to put her in such a state, but every time it ended the same. Roger had been both the threat and the savior, and the cycle kept repeating until the day he died. In her head she knew it was stupid, but in her heart she knew she'd done what he wanted every time. She'd researched it and read countless books; yet like the siren's call, she followed the same pattern, knowing she'd done it before and would do it again, and that again Roger had won.

She hadn't been able to stop the pattern, and she was a fool. Now, it had happened again. She'd fallen into the same trap, only it was a different person. Except Brendan hadn't done it on purpose. She could feel his remorse in the way he held her, so different than Roger. Roger had been stiff and upright, patting her on the back like a child, basking in his victory. Brendan was leaning over her, matching her shape with his, his cheek pressing into the top of her head as he nearly wrapped himself around her.

She should have felt frightened to be so consumed, but instead she felt completely safe, and she shouldn't have since he'd been the one to frighten her.

"Mommy?" Matthew's voice echoed from behind her. "What's wrong? Are you crying again?"

At the sound of the child's voice, Brendan released her. She turned around and bent down to speak to her son. "No," she said, pushing his hair off his face. "Mommy's not crying."

Brendan rammed his hands into his pockets. "I accidentally scared your mom. She didn't know I was here, so when the door opened, she thought I was a bad guy."

Matthew's eyes widened. "You mean she thought you was Uncle Ray coming to get stuff?"

A lump landed in Shanna's stomach. Of course, her children could see the tension between her and Ray, but she hadn't realized Matthew could be so perceptive. "Yes, I thought he was Uncle Ray. But it's just Mr. Brendan, so you can go back upstairs to your room."

He nodded. "I'll tell Ashley it's okay and she can come

out from under her bed," Matthew said and ran upstairs.

Shanna's world swirled around her, like the sensation of being sucked down into a whirling vortex from which there was no escape. "What have I done to my children?" she moaned.

"I don't understand."

"I've been fooling myself, trying to believe that they didn't know what was going on, first with Roger and now with Ray. My six-year-old son is coming down to see if I'm crying, and my four-year-old daughter is cowering under the bed. What kind of mother am I?"

"You're a mother who is doing her best to come out of a bad situation. Would you like me to explain what happened and assure them that something like that is never going to happen again?"

She turned to face him. "You'd do that?"

"Of course I would. I can't speak for what happened before, but today, this is my fault. I should have knocked or at least called out that it was me. I'll try to explain it to them. Their home should be a haven. I don't want them to feel insecure or unsafe."

All she could do was nod.

As she watched him go, she thought of what Roger would have done. Roger would have yelled at Matthew and told him to get back to his room, and he would have called Ashley a sissy, or worse, for hiding. Next he would have yelled at Shanna for causing him to lose his temper, commanded her to do something with her annoying children, then stomped out of the house and gone to the bar. It hadn't been until the day he died that Shanna found out that after going to the bar, he'd been going to another woman's house, and that was the reason he'd been coming home near sunrise. The night he died had been just like those other nights, except he hadn't made it to the other woman's house. It had been raining heavily, and in his drunken state, Roger had failed to negotiate a curve on the highway. His last words to Shanna had been that it was her fault that she had gotten him so angry, and that she was to blame for his drinking problem and his cheating on her.

She knew it wasn't her fault. Pastor Harry had helped her to believe that. Ray, on the other hand, told her almost every time he saw her those first few months that it was her fault his brother was dead.

Shanna wondered what Brendan thought.

A male voice sounded from the entrance to her office. "Hello, Shanna."

Shanna spun around. "Ray! What are you doing here?"

"You left the front door open," he sneered. "We're going to talk, and this time your sumo wrestler boyfriend isn't here." He stepped forward. Shanna backed up. "So what are you going to do?"

"Try anything, and she'll take you to court for assault," Brendan's voice echoed from behind Ray.

Ray spun around. "How did you get here?"

"That's not your concern. But I'll tell you something that is your concern. The last time you were here you left bruises. Shanna went to the clinic and had everything documented."

It took all of Shanna's strength and self-control, but she didn't back up. For once, she didn't move. She glared into Ray's eyes, forcing herself not to break eye contact when he glared back. "I also told the nurse about the bruises I see all the time on Evelyn's arms. I told them that my children were afraid of you. If you don't leave me alone, it's not too late to charge you with assault causing bodily harm."

His eyes narrowed. "You wouldn't do that. I'm family."

"Yes, I would, family or not."

Brendan stepped closer to Ray. "You've got a problem, Ray. You're the worst kind of bully. You don't just use threats and violence on strangers to get your way. You do it to people you're supposed to love, and who love you back, for reasons I will never understand. There are people who can help you." He reached into his back pocket for his wallet, pulled out a business card, and offered it to Ray. "Here's a place you can call that's completely anonymous. Don't just do it for your wife or for Shanna. Do it for yourself."

Ray didn't take the card. He ground out a string of curses that nearly curled Shanna's hair, then stomped out the way he came.

The second the front door slammed, Brendan unclipped his cell phone and punched in a phone number. "Evelyn? It's me, Brendan. Ray just left Shanna's, and he's plenty mad. I'd advise you to have your neighbor come to your house right now so you're not alone. Did you get my letter? Good. Let me know what happens." He snapped the phone closed and clipped it back onto his belt.

Shanna stared at him. "Why did you phone Evelyn? How did you get her number? What kind of letter are you talking about?"

"They have the same last name as you. I just looked it up in the phone book. I felt I had to get involved, so I phoned Evelyn. I told her that I knew what was going on in their house, and that it was only going to get worse. I also warned her that one day soon, Ray was going to leave here and go home really angry, and that she shouldn't be alone when that happens. I also asked for her permission to send her one of the cards that I just offered to Ray and a couple of brochures on spousal abuse."

Shanna's mouth dropped open.

"What he's doing is so wrong," Brendan continued. "God directs a husband to nourish and treasure his wife, not bully and mistreat her. God says that a man is to love his wife the way Christ loved the church. Christ loved the church so much He laid down his life for us, His church. Even when His people turned on Him, He healed the soldier's ear. He didn't strike back, even in self-defense. That's the way a man should treat his wife, as more important than anything, even his own life. Ray really needs to go to counseling. The place I suggested is free, anonymous, and without obligation."

Shanna stared at him. She wanted to believe that Brendan's words came from his heart. It was exactly what she wanted to hear, which meant it was too good to be true. How did he know what to say? He'd also said the exact right things to both Ray and Ray's wife. Giving a card as a reference they could use anytime was also a good thing to do, but Shanna wanted to know where Brendan had gotten the card. If he'd found the information from reading or by searching on the Internet, that was one thing. But if he had a card, that meant he'd been somewhere that had such cards readily available for men who needed help to control their violent tendencies.

He'd never been married. What if that was the reason?

She looked up at Brendan. She didn't think it would

ever happen, but she'd fallen in love with him. However, she'd been through the nightmare, and she wouldn't let it happen again. Before she got involved with Brendan, she had to be sure, without any doubt, that everything was right and as it should be. She still had doubt.

Shanna backed up. "What are you going to do now?"

He turned and stared at the empty doorway, the last place they'd seen Ray before he disappeared. "I don't trust him. I have a friend I think I'm going to call."

A friend.

It was always a friend. When Roger had briefly tried AA, that was what he said when he called his "someone else" who had the same problem but couldn't be identified. Someone she could never trace or talk to herself. Many times, after he'd gone to see his "friend," he'd come home drunker than he'd been before he left.

Without excusing himself or saying good-bye, Brendan turned and disappeared through the door from which he'd come, with Boffo following close behind, leaving Shanna alone in her office. He walked to the far corner of her yard, where she couldn't hear what he was saying, and spoke to someone on his cell phone.

The conversation was short. He was back in less than a minute.

"Can I borrow your car?"

"Where are you going?"

"I can't tell you."

Suddenly, she didn't want to know. She was too afraid.

The second she handed him the keys, he was gone.

eleven

Brendan parked his truck in front of Shanna's house, retrieved the last can of paint he would need, and walked into the backyard.

As always, Boffo ran to greet him. This time, though, as soon as he gave the dog his cursory pat, Boffo ran back to Brendan's mother, who was bound and determined that she was going to finish painting the fence today, no matter what.

The last part of his multilayered project, the fence, was done. Or it would be done, as soon as his mother finished painting it.

Shanna's yard had turned out to be one of his best contract projects. The seams in the sod were all grown together, and the yard was spectacular with the colors of a variety of roses, azaleas, and a couple of rhododendrons planted along the back fence. The two rock gardens he'd designed over the boulders he couldn't move were already awash with a rainbow of colors in the pansies and the flowing white and dark green of the low-growing alyssum.

Nearer to the house was the playscape, very different than his original plans. There was nothing more he could do to make it bigger or better. Any more, and he would probably need a building permit and to ask the city council for rezoning.

He'd even built a bird feeder and hung it in the back

corner. Already it had attracted the usual sparrows, as well as a few rose-breasted grosbeaks and various nuthatches. He'd also seen a couple of yellow finches close by, but not at the feeder, because they kept away from people.

Fortunately, he'd thought ahead and built it strong enough to withstand the weight of a pair of Steller's jays that came by almost every morning for a snack.

Brendan grinned as he remembered the first time Shanna had seen a Steller's jay so close. Most people, even those who lived here, called them blue jays, but they weren't. Blue jays had blue heads and crests, and they lived on the East Coast and toward the center of the continent. Steller's jays had black heads and crests and lived on the West Coast. Since they were a bit on the shy side for such a large bird, few people realized their size.

Under the eaves, on the back deck where he'd built a special lounger, he'd hung a hummingbird feeder. Even Boffo respected the tiny, brightly colored birds and their buzz of activity as they drank the red nectar, which he'd taught the children to make.

He looked into the corner of the yard at the doghouse. Or rather, the dog mansion. It was a perfect replica of the house, including a picture window, a shingled roof, and gutters, and it contained a king-sized dog bed that was raised off the ground. If only he could convince Boffo to use it.

In the back corner opposite the doghouse, he'd constructed a few collapsible hurdles, a line of poles for Boffo to weave through, a small bridge, a suspended hoop, and a cloth tunnel that he made out of heavy netting. The children had already devised a routine for it, although most of the time they ended up running through everything while Boffo sat and watched.

There was nothing more for Brendan to do. His job here was done.

He watched Shanna through the office window, sitting at her desk, concentrating intently on her work.

Ever since Ray's last visit, if it could be called a visit, she'd hardly spoken to Brendan, and he didn't know why. He'd done his best to act as a mediator, and as far as he knew, things were going well. Ray had promised to leave Shanna alone, and he'd finally agreed that he had no real claims on the car or anything else that used to belong to Roger. Brendan did notice Ray's failure to apologize to Shanna as promised, but he would take that one step at a time. The most important thing was that Ray had stopped bullying Shanna, and he said he would try counseling. Brendan prayed about it daily and would continue to do so, even if it took twenty years, although he hoped it wouldn't take that long for Ray to get his life sorted out.

Brendan walked to his mother and set the pail of paint on the ground beside her. "Here you go. The last one."

He straightened and was about to leave, but his mother grabbed his sleeve. "Wait. I have a surprise for you. Come with me."

She laid her paintbrush carefully on the tray and led Brendan into Shanna's office.

Shanna stop typing and looked up at him. "Is something wrong?"

"Nothing is wrong," Kathy chorused proudly. "But since everything is going to be finished this afternoon, I thought we should all take a little time and have a picnic for lunch."

Shanna leaned back in her chair and crossed her arms over her chest. "A what?"

"A picnic. I made a nice lunch for all of us this morning and packed it all up, ready to go. Everything is made, even a pitcher of nice cold iced tea." She made a great show of checking her wristwatch. "And it just happens to be lunchtime right now. Just let me cover up my painting things and we can go."

Shanna glanced back and forth between Brendan and his mother. Brendan knew better than to try to change his mother's mind or her plans.

"Go?" Shanna asked. "Go where?"

"We're going to go to the park at the community center. It's close but still away from home. Certainly you can spare half an hour."

"I. . ." Shanna's voice trailed off.

Brendan shrugged his shoulders. He wasn't going to argue with his mother. The surprise outing would give him a chance to talk to Shanna without distraction or interruption, since his mother was there and could watch the children.

Shanna sighed. "Okay. Maybe a break away from home is a good idea." She tapped a few more keys, hit SAVE, logged off, then copied her data to her flash drive and tucked it into her purse. "I'm ready."

Kathy scurried to her painting supplies, covered everything, closed the paint can, then pulled three backpacks out of the fort in the playscape. She helped the children with the two small ones and held the larger one out to Brendan.

"I guess we're walking," he muttered as he slung the

adult-sized pack over his shoulders and tucked his arms into the straps.

The children danced and skipped around Kathy, while Brendan kept a slower pace behind with Shanna.

Shanna didn't say anything, which he didn't think was good. Rather than dragging out the uncomfortable silence, Brendan struggled to fill all the empty airspace. He told her about his next big project, about some repairs he needed to do on his truck, about the things Boffo would learn when they signed him up for the agility team in the fall—anything that crossed his mind. It was the longest ten minutes of his life.

When they arrived at the park, he understood why the backpack had been so heavy. First, his mother pulled out a variety of containers containing different kinds of sandwiches, cut vegetables with dip, sliced fruit, three juice boxes, a coffee thermos, and a bin of chocolate chip cookies. After Shanna and Kathy arranged everything in the center of the blanket, Kathy allowed the children to empty their backpacks, which contained one sandwich and one juice box each.

"No cookies for you guys," Brendan teased. "I carried the cookies, so I get first dibs."

The children squealed, and when he laughed, Shanna elbowed him in the ribs.

The children ate quickly, then ran off to the swings, eating a cookie on their way. Shanna started to rise, but Kathy waved her hands in the air to keep Shanna seated. "Don't worry. I can push them. You stay here and relax."

Brendan's breath caught. He suddenly knew that his mother had planned this outing for this reason. One day soon, he would have to do something extra special for her.

"I heard from Evelyn today," Shanna said as she started to put the lids back on all his mother's lunch containers. "She told me that Ray has agreed to go to counseling and that he's already gone a couple of times. She told me to thank you for what you did."

"Not a problem. I did what I could."

She turned to him. "Why didn't you tell me where you were going when I gave you my car?"

"My friend told me not to tell anyone what I was doing in case there was a problem. If something went wrong, then the fewer people involved, the better. He said there could be liability issues."

"So you really did have a friend?"

Brendan quirked one eyebrow. "I have lots of friends."

Shanna's cheeks darkened. "I didn't mean it like that."

"I know. My friend is a social worker, and I'm not going to tell you his name. He's got to be careful about what he says and whom he's talking to. He especially has to be careful with unofficial advice. All I could do was summarize what happened as a hypothetical situation, and he could only make suggestions and tell me where the law will step in and where it won't. He warned me that things can sometimes get really ugly in domestic violence cases and that I shouldn't tell you what I was doing, just in case something really went bad. He was adamant that you definitely shouldn't be there. I can tell you a little about what happened because, for now, it looks like things are getting better. Ray hasn't hit Evelyn or made any threats against Evelyn, or against you, since the day he stormed out of your place. I don't know how a mind works in a situation like that, but something seemed to snap when I told him that he was a coward."

"A coward? I've always thought of him as a bully but never a coward."

"He's a coward if the only way he can get what he wants is by striking out at those who are smaller and weaker than himself, especially women, who seldom hit back. Think about it. He only picks a fight in situations where he can't possibly lose."

She looked up at him, her eyes wide.

"Don't do that," he mumbled. "I know what you're thinking. Most people are smaller and weaker than I am, and I know it. But I would never treat anyone that way. My mother raised me to treat people the way God would want me to. That's to treat others how I'd like them to treat me. With respect and dignity, and as an equal in God's sight."

She didn't respond, so he didn't say anything, either. Instead of talking, they simply watched the kids on the swings and his mother taking turns pushing them. A man joined them. His mother remained beside Ashley, while the man remained behind Matthew.

"That's my neighbor, John. Sometimes your mother talks to him over the fence while she's painting. It's so sad. His wife died just after Roger and I bought the house. About a year later his son moved out, and he's been all alone. I guess he keeps busy, but he's still alone."

"I know what you mean. My dad died when I was a kid, and I don't remember my mother dating back then. I know she's been out for dinner a few times with a few different men, more often lately, but nothing ever seems to work out. I don't know why. I wish she would get remarried.

She deserves to be happy."

Brendan's heart pounded, and he forced himself to breathe. He turned to Shanna, picked up one of her hands, and cradled it gently within his.

"You deserve to be happy, too, Shanna. I want to be the one to make you happy again, but something's happened. I feel like you've cut me off, and I don't know why."

She gulped and stared off into the distance, at her children. "It's hard to explain."

"Please try."

"It's not you. I don't know if I'm ready to think about relationships and stuff like that. I just want to concentrate on getting my business going and not neglect my kids."

"I'm not asking you to neglect your kids. What I want to do is spend more time with you, maybe something. . . uh"—Brendan swallowed, struggling to come up with the word—"permanent."

"Permanent?"

"Yes, permanent. Like married permanent. For life. Like until death do us part. Like getting old and gray together."

Her face paled. "Is this a proposal? Here? In the park?"

Gently, he massaged her hand. "Yes, it is. If you want, I can take you out for an expensive dinner, and I'll do it properly."

Her eyes widened and she stared at him.

"You can trust me to treat you the special way a man should treat the woman he loves." He lowered his voice. "I do love you, Shanna. And I love your kids, too. If you would marry me, I'd want to adopt them as my own." He gave her a weak grin. "Boffo, too. I just won't go so far as to say I love him, but I do like him."

She didn't smile at his little joke. "I need to think about it. I didn't expect this. Whenever a man asks a woman to marry him, before that happens, she's already expecting it. I didn't."

"It's okay. Take all the time you need."

But really, it wasn't okay. Inside, a little piece of him died. He hadn't expected her to turn cartwheels, but he had expected a more positive reaction—and certainly something more encouraging.

Shanna leaned forward and started to tuck all the containers back into the backpack. "I think it's time for me to get back to work, and you, too."

She handed him the backpack, and they both stood. Together they folded the blanket; then Shanna tucked it into the backpack and fastened it closed.

His mother didn't need signal flares. As soon as she saw them packing up, she got the children off the swings and brought them back to the picnic area, with Shanna's neighbor at her side. Shanna introduced the men to each other, and soon the group was on their way.

Brendan didn't say anything as he walked beside Shanna. He didn't know what to say. Even though things weren't going the way he wanted them to, he could understand that it was a big decision for her, even bigger because she had lived on the bad side of marriage. She didn't know how good it could be. He knew, because he'd seen it in his parents' marriage—a marriage that had ended much too soon.

He could only take solace in knowing that he'd done what he thought God wanted him to do, and that was to show Shanna how much he loved her. He'd done that by protecting her as best he could, which put him at substantial risk. His friend Sal, the social worker, had warned him that Ray could snap and strike out at him, and it wasn't uncommon for weapons to be involved.

Ray was a gun owner, which didn't come as a surprise. Fortunately, Ray's wife was much smarter than Ray gave her credit for. When Brendan called to warn her that Ray was on the way, she'd hidden Ray's guns, knowing the potential, and she'd locked his dog, Killer, in the backyard. Ray had picked up the fireplace poker to go after Evelyn but had then turned on Brendan when he burst in on them. God truly had been at work in Ray and Evelyn's house that day, because everything Sal had warned him about had happened. The good news was that Brendan managed to calm Ray down and get the poker away from him before any harm was done. Then, after a lot of careful talking, Ray actually listened to Brendan. He'd taken everything Brendan said to heart and was now working on controlling his anger.

Too soon, they arrived back at Shanna's house.

Since he didn't have anything more to say, Brendan simply climbed into his truck and drove away to his next job site, knowing it was going to be a very long day.

❧

Shanna stared at her computer screen without doing anything for so long that her screen saver came on.

She sat there mesmerized by the little fish swimming back and forth, complete with bubbles and the odd, exploding blowfish.

She managed to snap her brain back into wanting to do some work and was just about to hit a key to deactivate the screen saver when the phone rang.

She looked at the time. It was after 8:00, and the children were already in bed. Whoever was calling, it wasn't business.

Her hand froze over the receiver before she picked it up. If it was Brendan, she didn't know what she would say.

She hadn't been fair to him. She should have told him that she was afraid, but her reason for being afraid wasn't fair to him, either. He was a good and valiant man. When Shanna knew Ray had left for work, she'd phoned Evelyn and asked for more details of what happened the day Brendan had stepped into the middle of the situation. What she heard wasn't pretty.

Brendan had done his research—both on trying to understand what she was going through and on what Ray would be going through—then stepped into the middle, putting himself at risk. And he'd done it for her.

On the sixth ring, she finally picked up the phone.

"Shanna? It's me, Kathy. I'm sorry for phoning so late, but I wanted to ask you a question about your neighbor John."

"What do you want to know?" she asked, knowing her voice sounded almost squeaky.

"Are you okay? Your voice sounds funny."

"I'm fine," Shanna replied, knowing she didn't sound fine.

"Would you like to tell me what's wrong?"

Shanna cringed. Her voice came out in a hoarse croak. "Can I ask you a really personal question?" she whispered.

"Anything you want," Kathy said, sounding hesitant.

Shanna steeled her nerve. "Did you and your husband ever fight?"

Kathy paused. "It depends on what you mean by 'fight.'

I hope you don't mind, but Matthew told me a little bit about your brother-in-law. Matthew is scared of him because you're scared of him. So I'm going to assume that when you say 'fight,' you don't mean 'argue.' Gerry and I argued, but we never hit each other, and we never threw things. I won't say we never raised our voices, but we always worked it out. Does that help?"

Shanna thought of all she'd been through with Roger and what she'd seen with her parents. Kathy's experience had been the complete opposite of her own. Which meant it was possible for her to have the same.

"Yes, that does help. Can I ask you something else?"

"Anything."

"Did your husband let you win any of those arguments?"

"Let me win? I'm not sure what to say. No one ever won or lost. We worked everything out until we came to some kind of agreement. Neither of us ever 'let' the other win, and nothing was a contest where there was a winner and a loser. It was more the other way around. Sometimes I gave in; sometimes he did, but most of the time we met in the middle. It wasn't over until both of us could live with the decision. But we didn't argue very often. In a good marriage, both partners usually think along the same lines in the things that are important. Family, children, money, daily life matters. . . The things we argued about were the nonessentials. Furniture colors. Cars. Stupid things, looking back. Often we'd just laugh about it later. And then we'd—uh, never mind. What were you saying?"

Shanna remembered Brendan's words, and they echoed what his mother had said, in a different way. Marriage was a partnership.

Her parents' marriage hadn't been a partnership. It was her father's way or no way. When she first started dating, her mother had told her that it didn't matter about winning or losing, probably because she never won. Her mother said what mattered was that a woman had to find a husband who would have her for better or worse. Except that her father hadn't stuck around for better or worse. He'd left for something better.

She didn't have any examples of a good marriage in her family or in her own life. The only thing Shanna knew about what a marriage was supposed to be like was what she'd read or heard from the people she knew at church. Brendan had lived with good examples, and he still believed the same things and held the same values. He probably always would.

He would never strike out in anger. It wasn't in him to do so, both by his nature and by the examples and teaching he'd grown up with. The way he'd dealt with Ray was proof of that. He would never bully or badger her or the children, and he would always be fair. And as he said, he would always love her; and to him, love meant a partnership. She couldn't ask for more than that.

"I'm sorry. What did you want to know about John?"

"What's he like? He asked me out to dinner, and I didn't know what to say."

"I don't see him that much, but I usually see him at least on Sundays, because we go to the same church. Sometimes we go together, but not always, because of the kids. The kids like him, too. I don't know him really well, but he seems very nice."

Shanna leaned forward and peeked through the blinds.

Speaking of John, she couldn't see him, exactly, but the light was on in the family room, and she detected flickers indicating the television was on, and she could see occasional movements. Even though she didn't know what he was doing, she knew he was awake and alone.

"Thanks," Kathy said. "That's exactly what I wanted to know. I'll catch you next Tuesday, for Ladies' Night at my church. Are you still interested?"

"Yes. Very much. Thanks for calling, and I really mean that."

The second she hung up, she dialed John's phone number.

"Hi, John. It's Shanna, next door. This is nothing urgent, but I was wondering if you could come over and keep an eye on the kids for a while. They're in bed, but I have to go out and get something. I'd owe you, big-time."

John laughed through the phone. "You know I'm not doing anything important. I'll be right there."

She scribbled down the address from her files, grabbed her purse, and ran to the door.

By the time John's foot touched the first step, Shanna was already on the porch. "I'll be back in an hour, tops, not a minute longer. I promise," she chorused as she closed the car door.

In record time, she had arrived at Brendan's town house.

The door opened. In some ways, he looked exactly the same as he always did, but also entirely different.

Since he'd gotten his hair cut, he'd continued to shave every day, but she could understand what he'd said about his reasons for his former style, or lack thereof. After his new haircut, he'd gelled it up, and he had been keeping that up daily, as well as continuing to shave diligently. But now, later in the evening, he had obviously showered and washed all the gel out and not bothered to use more since he was home alone. His hair was now half flopped over on his head and half sticking out all over because it wasn't combed. And he hadn't been kidding when he'd said his five o'clock shadow started at two o'clock. It was now nearly eight thirty, and his chin was as scruffy as the "didn't shave for a day and a half" look of some of the tough-guy movie stars. Only she knew Brendan didn't work to achieve the look; it was just the way he was.

He was wearing a freshly laundered T-shirt. But if it hadn't been for the fresh-from-the-dryer scent of his fabric softener she wouldn't have been able to tell it was clean, because it was stained with paint of a dozen different colors. Likewise, his jeans. They were so old they were nearly white. From age and perhaps hundreds of wearings, they were worn thin in places, especially on the knees—one of which was ripped all the way through. If she wasn't mistaken, she saw a few different colors of paint on his jeans, too.

She was curious to see if his socks would be in the same condition as the rest of his clothes, but his feet were bare.

Even though Shanna was wearing her shoes and he had nothing to add to his height, he still towered over her.

She looked up. Way up. Just as she had the first time they met.

His cheeks darkened. "This is a surprise."

She held up a fast-food bag. "I brought food."

One eyebrow quirked. "Food? But"—he checked his watch—"it's a little late for supper, isn't it?" He peeked over her shoulder with no effort. "Where are the kids?"

"They're in good hands. May I come in?"

His cheeks darkened even more, all the way to his ears. "I'm sorry for being rude. I wasn't expecting you. Come in."

He stepped aside and then closed the door behind her.

She had never been to his home before, but it was exactly as she had pictured it would be. There was no sense of coordination or décor, yet for the all the mismatches, everything fit together to make a warm and cozy home. Fluffy cushions were strewn haphazardly on the biggest couch she'd ever seen. The coffee table was piled with newspapers, magazines, and a few fiction books, one spread open for lack of a bookmark, as was his Bible, the same one she'd seen him with in church.

Taking a guess, she headed in the direction of where she thought the kitchen would be.

She bit her bottom lip as she passed his bedroom, complete with an unmade bed and the clothes she'd seen him wearing earlier that day, lying in a pile on the floor.

He'd had a home-cooked meal; she could tell, because he hadn't yet done the dishes. The dishwasher was wide open, still half filled with clean dishes waiting to be put away.

"I wasn't expecting company," Brendan muttered behind her. "What are you doing here?"

"I only had twenty dollars on me, so this was the best I could do on short notice. But if you want, I can take you out tomorrow for an expensive dinner and do this properly."

She heard his sharp intake of breath. "Please tell me you mean what I think you mean."

She walked to him and rested her hands on the sides of his waist. "That's exactly what I mean. I love you, and I'd be the happiest woman in the world if you'd marry me and my little family. If the offer is still open."

His answer came in the form of a kiss, immediate, passionate, and all-consuming.

And she kissed him back in exactly the same way.

The hamburgers and fries never did get eaten. By the time they separated, she didn't have time to sit down. She had to rush back home so John could go home and get to bed. After all, he had to go to work in the morning.

"Wait." Brendan raised his hand and rested it on the door, keeping it closed. "Not that I think you'd change your mind, but when is this going to happen?"

Shanna shrugged her shoulders. "I hadn't thought that far in advance."

Brendan cupped her face with his hands and brushed a gentle kiss across her lips. "I don't believe in long engagements. How about setting a date for Harry's first open weekend?"

Her heart nearly burst with joy. "I could do that. I guess this means you want to get married at my church, not your own?"

His hands slid down to her shoulders. "I don't know; I think it would be a tough decision. But I have an idea for meeting in the middle. Instead of having to decide between the two, let's get married in the place we met."

"The place we met?" She pictured clearly the first time she met him. Pastor Harry had brought Brendan to her home so he could give her an estimate. "We met for the first time in my backyard."

"Yeah. Your backyard. There's plenty of room, and you've got to admit, your landscaper did a mighty fine job. It would be perfect for a summer wedding."

Shanna giggled. "I think I'll have to give that man a big, big bonus."

"I'm sure he can hardly wait," he said, then kissed her again.

Her yard would indeed be perfect.

epilogue

A slight breeze rippled through Pastor Harry's hair, which Shanna thought a perfect touch for a perfect day. Usually there wasn't much wind around Seattle, but today was warm, and the slight breeze was refreshing.

"Mom! Come on! It's time!"

Shanna smiled. They had planned to keep the guest list small because the wedding would be very informal and there would be limited seating capacity in her backyard. In keeping with a small guest list, they'd chosen only one attendant each. Since Brendan couldn't have the pastor who was presiding over the ceremony be his best man, he'd asked his friend Thomas, who just happened to be the same man who had delivered and helped lay the sod they were standing on. It was only fitting that he should be part of the ceremony.

Shanna had chosen her daughter to be her maid of honor, a responsibility that Ashley had taken very seriously. Since Shanna hadn't seen her father since her teenage years, she wanted the other man who was important to her to give her away, and that would be her son, Matthew.

Shanna patted a stray lock of hair into place and smiled at her son. "I'm ready. We can go now."

"Mom, before we go, Ashley and I have a surprise for you."

Ashley stood by the door, shuffling her feet, indicating to Shanna that something wasn't quite right.

Shanna's smile faltered. She didn't want any surprises today, her wedding day.

Outside, the music changed to the wedding march.

Matthew led her one step outside then stopped. He pointed to Boffo, who was wearing a black collar, and a tie hung where his dog tags should have been. In his mouth he held a small basket with a pillow nested inside.

The ring bearer pillow.

Shanna gasped. "Boffo can't be in the wedding party!"

Ashley giggled. "Me and Matthew been training him, just like you and Mr. Brendan." Ashley's giggle turned into a very serious frown. "Is we allowed to call Mr. Brendan 'Daddy' now? I think he's gonna make a great daddy."

Shanna looked to the front of the yard, where Brendan and Thomas stood waiting.

Even though the wedding was the most informal one Shanna had ever been to, Brendan was still a nervous groom. From across the yard, she could see one knee shaking, and he kept wiping his hands down the sides of his slacks.

"Yes. Brendan is going to make a fine daddy for you two. Now let's get going and make this wedding happen so he can be your daddy."

Ashley stiffened, blinked her eyes, then turned, ready to walk forward as they'd practiced.

"Okay, Boffo. You can give our new daddy the rings now! Go!"

The children had given Boffo the right idea, but the excited dog didn't know the meaning of the word *slow*. He bounded through the yard, circled the playscape, took a running jump over one of the rock gardens, then ran full speed to Brendan. Unable to contain his excitement, with so many people in his yard, Boffo ran in circles around Brendan, all the while still holding the basket in his mouth.

"Boffo, sit," Brendan commanded calmly.

Boffo sat. Quickly, Brendan removed the basket from the dog's mouth, set it on the side of Pastor Harry's portable podium, and gave Boffo the signal to lie down, which Boffo did.

A few people snickered quietly, while Shanna thought she'd faint with relief.

Since everything was quiet, everyone turned and watched her and the children, including Brendan.

And then Brendan winked.

All her nervousness dissolved. The man she loved was waiting patiently for her.

Shanna smiled. "Come on, Ashley, Matthew. Let's go."

Ashley walked beautifully in front of them, and Matthew very solemnly escorted Shanna to stand beside Brendan and in front of Pastor Harry. Just like a real man, he smiled up at Brendan, gave Brendan a brief nod of approval, then stepped back.

Because of the outside setting, they'd planned the ceremony to be very brief, and it was. During the short ceremony, Boffo remained still, lying as he had been instructed, at Brendan's feet. He rose and sat, watching intently as they exchanged the rings, which brought smiles to everyone present, especially when Ashley started to giggle. They signed the register, and Pastor Harry had just begun to address the guests with his benediction when Boffo decided he wanted the basket with the ring bearer's pillow back.

He raised one paw and scratched at the podium to signal his intentions.

Pastor Harry cringed, then kept talking to the guests.

"Boffo, no," Shanna whispered, then smiled at Pastor Harry.

Boffo scratched the podium again, this time with an added whine.

"What is he doing?" she whispered to Brendan.

"I have no idea," Brendan replied, also in a hushed whisper.

Boffo rose up on his back legs, leaning with his front legs high on the podium, his nose inches from the basket.

"Boffo! Down!" Shanna ground out between her teeth, trying to make everyone think she was just smiling, but Boffo didn't listen.

Ashley tugged on Shanna's skirt. "Mommy, Matthew and me put a doggie cookie under the pillow so he wouldn't put it down and lose your pretty new ring."

"Oh, no. . ." Shanna reached out to snag the basket, but when Boffo saw her going for it, he moved so fast it was as if he'd sprouted wings. The huge dog sprang forward to get it first, banging into the podium. It tottered, then began to tip.

Brendan made a grab for the podium, but he couldn't reach it fast enough without knocking Matthew over.

The podium fell onto the end of the table where Kathy had set a few flower arrangements. With one end of the table going down, the other acted like a catapult, flinging the flowers into the air, pots and all. The women in the front dashed forward, scrambling to catch the flying flowers before the vases shattered on the ground. The men lunged to catch Shanna's boom box and detached speakers, which were now airborne.

Boffo jumped high into the air, caught the basket, then

ran helter-skelter among the displaced guests, clearly proud of himself for capturing his prize.

Ashley squeaked and pointed at Boffo, following everywhere he ran. Matthew ran behind Boffo, yelling Boffo's name while trying to catch him.

"I now pronounce you man and wife!" Pastor Harry yelled over the mayhem. "Brendan! Please kiss the bride!"

Brendan nudged Shanna to step away from the center of the action.

Shanna looked up at Brendan. "I love you so much."

Brendan drew her into his embrace. "I"—Brendan jerked as Boffo sideswiped him then kept going—"love you, too. And your kids. But I'll get back to you on the dog."

A Letter To Our Readers

Dear Reader:
In order that we might better contribute to your reading enjoyment, we would appreciate your taking a few minutes to respond to the following questions. We welcome your comments and read each form and letter we receive. When completed, please return to the following:

Fiction Editor
Heartsong Presents
PO Box 719
Uhrichsville, Ohio 44683

1. Did you enjoy reading *Love by the Yard* by Gail Sattler?
   ❏ Very much! I would like to see more books by this author!
   ❏ Moderately. I would have enjoyed it more if

   _____

   _____

   _____

2. Are you a member of **Heartsong Presents**?   ❏ Yes   ❏ No
   If no, where did you purchase this book? _____

   _____

3. How would you rate, on a scale from 1 (poor) to 5 (superior), the cover design? _____

4. On a scale from 1 (poor) to 10 (superior), please rate the following elements.

   ____ Heroine   ____ Plot
   ____ Hero   ____ Inspirational theme
   ____ Setting   ____ Secondary characters

5. These characters were special because? _____

_____

_____

6. How has this book inspired your life? _____

_____

_____

7. What settings would you like to see covered in future
   Heartsong Presents books? _____

_____

_____

8. What are some inspirational themes you would like to see
   treated in future books? _____

_____

_____

9. Would you be interested in reading other **Heartsong
   Presents** titles? ❏ Yes ❏ No

10. Please check your age range:
     ❏ Under 18   ❏ 18-24
     ❏ 25-34   ❏ 35-45
     ❏ 46-55   ❏ Over 55

Name _____

Occupation _____

Address _____

City, State, Zip_____

Sugar and Grits

4 stories in 1

Southern hospitality enriches four Mississippi romances.

Houston, Texas, authors DiAnn Mills, Martha Rogers, Janice Thompson, and Kathleen Y'Barbo have used their appreciation of small-town life to create this engaging collection.

Historical, paperback, 352 pages, 5³⁄₁₆" x 8"

Heart❤ng

Any 12 Heartsong Presents titles for only $27.00*

CONTEMPORARY ROMANCE IS CHEAPER BY THE DOZEN!

Buy any assortment of twelve *Heartsong Presents* titles and save 25% off the already discounted price of $2.97 each!

*plus $3.00 shipping and handling per order and sales tax where applicable.
If outside the U.S. please call 740-922-7280 for shipping charges.

HEARTSONG PRESENTS TITLES AVAILABLE NOW:

(If ordering from this page, please remember to include it with the order form.)